Mary Cholmondeley

A devotee: An episode in the life of a butterfly

Mary Cholmondeley

A devotee: An episode in the life of a butterfly

ISBN/EAN: 9783743373600

Manufactured in Europe, USA, Canada, Australia, Japa

Cover: Foto ©Andreas Hilbeck / pixelio.de

Manufactured and distributed by brebook publishing software (www.brebook.com)

Mary Cholmondeley

A devotee: An episode in the life of a butterfly

A DEVOTEE

An Episode in the Life of a Butterfly

MARY CHOLMONDELEY

AUTHOR OF

'DIANA TEMPEST,' 'SIR CHARLES DANVERS,' AND 'THE
DANVERS JEWELS'

SECOND EDITION

EDWARD ARNOLD

LONDON   NEW YORK
37 BEDFORD STREET   70 FIFTH AVENUE

1897

All rights reserved

To

FLORIE,

UPON WHOSE KIND STRONG HAND

I HAVE SO OFTEN LEANT.

855

'That day is sure,
Though not perhaps this week, nor month, nor year,
When your great love shall clean forgotten be,
And my poor tenderness shall yet endure.'

WILFRID S. BLUNT.

A DEVOTEE.

CHAPTER I.

'Yet to be loved makes not to love again ;
Not at my years, however it hold in youth.'
TENNYSON.

THE cathedral was crammed. The tall
slender arches seemed to spring out of a
vast sea of human heads. The orchestra
and chorus had gradually merged into one
person : one shout of praise, one voice of
prayer, one wail of terror. The *Elijah*
was in mid-career, sailing like a man-of-
war upon the rushing waves of music.

And presently there was a hush, and out of the hush a winged voice arose, as a lark rises out of a meadow, singing as it rises :

' O rest in the Lord, wait patiently for Him, and He shall give thee thy heart's desire.'

The lark dropped into its nest again. The music swept thundering upon its way, and a large tear fell unnoticed from a young girl's eyes on to the bare slim hand which held her score. The score quivered ; the slender willowy figure quivered in its setting of palest violet and white draperies threaded with silver. Only a French-woman could have dared to translate a child's posy of pale blue and white violets, tied with a silver string, into a gown ; but Sibyl Carruthers' dressmaker was an artist in her way, and took an artist's

license, and the half-mourning which she
had designed for the great heiress was
in colouring what a bereaved butterfly
might have worn.

Miss Carruthers was called beautiful.
Perhaps she was beautiful for an heiress,
but she was certainly not, in reality, any
prettier than many hundreds of dowerless
girls who had never been considered more
than good-looking.

Her delicate features were too irregular,
in spite of their obvious high breeding ;
her figure was too slight ; her complexion
was too faintly tinted for regular beauty.
But she had something of the evanescent
charm of a four-petalled dog-rose newly
blown—exquisite, ethereal, but as if it might
fall in a moment. This aspect of fragility
was heightened by what women noticed
about her first, namely, her gossamer

gown with its silver gleam, and by what men noticed about her first—her gray eyes, pathetic, eager, shy by turns, always lovely, but hinting of a sword too sharp for its slender sheath, of an ardent spirit whose grasp on this world was too slight.

And as the music passed over her young untried soul, she sat motionless, her hands clasping the score. She heard nothing of it, but it accompanied the sudden tempest of passion which was shaking her, as wind accompanies storm.

The voice of the song had stirred an avalanche of emotion.

'And I will give thee thy heart's desire.'

She knew nothing about waiting patiently, but her heart's desire—she must have it. She could not live without it. Her whole soul went out in an agony of prayer to the God who gives and who

withholds to accord her this one petition—
to be his wife. She repeated it over and
over again. To be near him, to see him
day by day—nothing else, nothing else!
This one thing, without which, poor child!
she thought she could not live. It seemed
to Sibyl that she was falling at God's
feet in the whirlwind, and refusing to let
Him go until He granted her prayer.
But would He grant it? Her heart sank.
Despair rushed in upon her like a flood
at the bare thought of its refusal, and she
caught yet again at the only hope left to
her—a desperate appeal to the God who
gives and who withholds.

Presently it was all over, and they were
going out.

'We were to wait for the others here,'
said Peggy, the girl who had been sitting
with Sibyl, as they emerged into the sun-

shine with the crowd. 'Mother and Mr. Doll were just behind us.'

Lady Pierpoint, Sibyl's aunt, presently joined them with Mr. Doll Loftus, an irreproachable - looking, unapproachable-looking fair young man, who, it was whispered, was almost too smart to live, but who nevertheless bore himself with severe simplicity.

He went up to Sibyl with some diffidence.

'You are tired,' he said anxiously.

Doll's remarks were considered *banal* in the extreme by some women, but others who admired fair hair and pathetic eyes found a thoughtful beauty in them.

It would be difficult from her manner to infer which class of sentiments this particular remark awoke in Sibyl.

'Music always tires me,' she replied,

without looking at him, dropping her white eyelids.

'Are we all here?' said Lady Pierpoint. 'Peggy, and Sibyl—my dear, how tired you look!—and myself, and you, Mr. Doll; that is only four, and "we are seven." Ah! here come Mr. and Mrs. Cathcart. Now we only want Mr. Loftus.'

'The Dean caught him in the doorway,' said Doll. 'He is coming now.'

The tall thin figure of an elder man was slowly crossing the angular patch of sunshine where the cathedral had not cast its great shadow. The nobility of his bearing seemed to appeal to the crowd. They made way for him instinctively, as if he were some distinguished personage. He was accompanied by a robust clerical figure with broad calves.

'Mr. Loftus makes everyone else look

common,' said Peggy plaintively. 'It is the only unkind thing I know about him. I thought the Dean quite dignified-looking while we were at luncheon at the Deanery, but now he looks like a pork-butcher. I'm not going to walk within ten yards of Mr. Loftus, mummy, or I shall be taken for a parlourmaid having her day out. I think, Sibyl, you are the only one who can afford to go with him.'

But Doll thought differently, and it was he and Sibyl who walked the short distance to the station together through the flag-decked streets in the brilliant September sunshine. People turned to glance at them as they passed. They made a striking-looking couple. Mr. Loftus, fol-lowing slowly at a little distance with Lady Pierpoint, looked affectionately at the back of his young cousin, who was also his heir, and said to her, with a smile :

'I wish it could be. Doll is a good fellow.'

'I wish indeed it could,' said Lady Pierpoint earnestly, with the slight slackening of reserve which is often observable in the atmosphere on the last afternoon of a visit with a purpose.

Lady Pierpoint had not come to spend a whole week with a Sunday in it with Mr. Loftus at Wilderleigh for nothing. And she was aware that neither had she and her niece and daughter been invited for that long period without a cause. But the week ended with the following morning, and she sighed. She had daughters of her own coming on, as well as her dear snub-nosed Peggy, who was already out, and it was natural to wish that the re-

sponsibility of this delicate, emotional
creature, with her great wealth, might be
taken from her and placed in safe hands.
She thought Doll was safe. Perhaps the
wish was father, or rather *aunt*, to the
thought. But it was no doubt the truest
epithet that could be applied to the young
man. It was a matter of opinion whether
he was exhaustingly dull in conversation or
extraordinarily interesting, but he certainly
was safe. He belonged to that class of
our latter-day youth of whom it may be pre-
dicted, with some confidence, that they will
never cause their belongings a moment's
uneasiness ; who may be trusted never to
do anything very right or very wrong ;
who will get on tolerably well in any
position, and with any woman, provided
there are means to support it and—*her ;*
who have enough worldliness to marry

money, and enough good feeling to make irreproachable husbands afterwards ; in short, the kind of young men who are invented by Providence on purpose to marry heiresses, and who, if they fall below their vocation, dwindle, when their youth is over, into the padded impecunious bores of society.

There was a short journey by rail through the hop country. Sibyl watched the rows of hops in silence. Cowardice has its sticking-point as well as courage, and she was undergoing the miserable preliminary tremors by which that point is reached. Mr. Loftus, sitting opposite her, and observing her fixity of gaze, glanced at her rather wistfully from time to time. He saw something was working in her mind. He looked tired, and in the strong afternoon light his grave, lined face seemed more worn and world-weary than ever. He had the look of a man who had long outlived all personal feeling, and who to-day had been remembering his youth.

The Wilderleigh omnibus and Doll's spider-wheeled dogcart were waiting at the little roadside station, which was so small that the train very nearly overlooked it, and had to be backed. Doll was already holding the wheel to protect Sibyl's gown as she got up, and looking towards her, and Lady Pierpoint was hurrying Peggy, who had expressed a hankering after the dogcart, into the omnibus, when Mr. Loftus observed that he thought he would walk up.

Sibyl's face changed.

' May I walk up with you ?' she asked instantly.

Mr. Loftus looked disappointed ; every-body looked disappointed. Lady Pierpoint put her head out, and said :

' My dear child, the drive in the open air will refresh you ; you are looking tired.'

' May I go in the dogcart if Sibyl doesn't want to ?' put in Peggy in an audible aside to her mother.

' I think you are tired,' said Mr. Loftus, looking at Sibyl and shaking his head. ' And,' he added in a lower voice, ' Doll will be much disappointed.'

A faint colour covered her face, which quivered as she turned it towards him.

' Let me walk up with you,' she said again, with a tremor in her voice.

He met her appealing eyes with gentle scrutiny.

' It is not far,' he said aloud ; ' not more than half a mile through the park. I will take care of her, Lady Pierpoint. We shall be at Wilderleigh almost as soon as you are.'

'Oh, mummy, may I go in the dogcart *now* ?' implored Peggy from the depths of the omnibus.

And Mr. Loftus and Sibyl set out together.

They were in the park in a few minutes, and were walking down towards Wilderleigh, on the opposite side of the river, an old house of weather-beaten gray stone, of twisted chimneys and uneven roofs and pointed gables, with quaint carved finials, standing above its terraces and its long stone balustrade. The sun was setting in a sky of daffodil behind the tall top-heavy elms of the rookery and the tower of the village church. Little fleets of clouds lay motionless in high heaven, looking towards the west. The land in its long shadows dreamed of peace. The old house beyond the river was in shadow already. So was the river.

'Sometimes,' said Mr. Loftus to himself, 'a young girl feels more able to confide in an old friend than a relation. She has often talked to me before. Perhaps she is going to do so again.' And he felt comforted about Doll and the dogcart.

Presently as he glanced at her, wondering at her continued silence, he saw that she was greatly agitated.

'Something troubles you,' he said gently.

She looked at him half in terror, as if deprecating his anger.

They were walking down a narrow ride in the tall bracken. A trunk of a tree lay near the path among the yellowing fern.

He led her to it and sat down by her, looking at her with painful anxiety and with a sense of growing fatigue. Emotion of any kind exhausted him. If it had not been for Doll, he would have dropped the subject, but for his sake he made an effort.

'Tell me,' he said, and he took her thin young hand and held it in his thin older hand. It was the last afternoon; both were conscious of it.

She trembled very much, but she did not speak. His heart sank.

'You wish to tell me something about Doll, perhaps,' he said at last. 'Do not be afraid of paining me by talking of it. You like him, perhaps, but not enough, and you are grieved because you see how much he loves you. Is that it?'

'I don't like him,' gasped Sibyl. 'I have

never thought about it. That is only
Aunt Marion.'

Mr. Loftus sighed, and his gray cheek
blanched a little. He had built much on
the hope of this marriage. He had a
tender regard for Sibyl, whose emotional
and impulsive nature appealed to him, and
filled him with apprehension as for a
butterfly in a manufactory, which may
injure itself any moment. And he knew
Doll was genuinely in love with her. It
would be grievous if she were married for
her money. And Wilderleigh was dying
stone by stone and acre by acre for want
of that money.

As he looked mournfully at Sibyl, an
expression came into her wide eyes like
that which he had seen in the eyes of some
timid wild animal brought to bay. He
recognised that, like a shy bird near its

nest, she was defending in impotent despair of broken white wings something which was part of her life, which was going from her, which *he* was taking away.

'It is you I love,' she said, and her small hand ceased trembling and became cold in his.

For a moment both were stunned alike, and then some of the grayness of age and suffering crept suddenly from his face to hers as she felt his hand involuntarily slacken its clasp of hers.

'My child,' he said at last, with great difficulty and with greater tenderness, 'it is very many years since I gave up all thought of marriage. I am old enough to be your——' He might have said 'grandfather' with truth. He meant to say it, but as he approached the word he could not wound her with it.

'I know,' she interrupted hurriedly. . 'I don't mind. That is nothing to me.'

'And my life,' he said, 'what little there is left of it, hangs by a thread.'

'I know,' she said again—'I have thought of that. I have thought of nothing but you since I first met you a year ago. But if I might only love and serve you and be with you! And I am so rich, too. If I might only take away those money troubles which you once spoke of long ago! If I might only give you everything I have! The money is the smallest part of it—oh, such a little, little part com-pared to——' And she looked imploringly at him.

He was deeply moved.

'My child,' he said again, and the ominous repetition of the word shook her fragile edifice of hopes to its brittle foundation, 'you have always looked upon me as a friend, have you not?'

She shook her head.

'Well, then,' he added, correcting himself, 'as one who cared for and understood you, and whose earnest wish was to see you happy?'

She did not answer.

He had known difficult hours, but none more difficult than this. He felt as if he were trying with awkward hands to hold a butterfly without injuring it, in order to release it from the pane of glass against which it was beating its butterfly heart out.

'To see you happy,' he went on, with authority as well as tenderness in his level voice. 'I should never see that; I should have no real'—he hesitated—'affection for you at all if I allowed you to make such a woeful mistake in your early youth before you know what love and life are. They are terrible things, Sibyl ; I have known them. This beautiful generous feeling which you have for me is not love, and I should be base indeed to allow you to wreck your life upon it, your youth upon the rock of my age. You offer you know not what ; you would sacrifice you know not what.' He smiled gravely at her, endeavouring to soothe her growing agitation. 'It would be like taking the Koh-i-Noor out of the hand of a child. I could not do it.'

Her mind was in too great a tumult wholly to understand him, but one thing was clear to her, namely, that he was refusing to marry her. She snatched her hands out of his, and, starting wildly to her feet with an inarticulate cry, ran a short distance and flung herself down on her face among the bracken.

He looked after her, but he did not follow her. He could do no more, and a sense of exhaustion and distress was upon him. He had been clumsy. He had hurt the poor butterfly, after all.

He sat a long time on the tree-trunk, the low sunshine on his worn, patient face, on which the refinement of suffering and of thought had set their indelible stamp. And now the thin high features wore a new look of present distress over the old outlived troubles, a new look which anyone who really loved him would have been heart-stricken to have called into it. But when love ceases to wound its object, and bears its own cross, it has ceased to be young.

As he sat motionless the sun sank.

Far in the amber west the heavens had opened in an agony of glory. The knotted arms of the great oaks, upraised like those of Moses and his brethren, shone red as flame against the darkness of the forest. The first hint of chill after the great heat came into the still air.

Mr. Loftus rose and went slowly towards the prostrate figure in its delicate gleaming gown.

' Sibyl,' he said gently, but with authority, 'you must get up. I see Doll and your cousin coming up the glade to meet us.'

Sibyl started violently and raised herself, turning a white, hopeless face towards him. Her entire self-abandonment, which would have brought acute humiliation to another woman, brought none to her. Her despair was too complete to admit of any other feeling.

'Like a child's,' he thought, as he looked at her sorrowing.

He helped her to smooth her gown, and he set her hat straight, and took some pieces of dried bracken out of her crumpled shining hair. She let him do it, neither helping nor hindering him. She evidently did not care what impression might be made on the minds of the two young people leisurely approaching them. She would have lain on the ground if it had been a bog instead of dry turf until the ice fit of despair had passed. His thoughtfulness for her, and the ashen tint of his face, were nothing to her, any more than the moonshine is to the child who has cried for the moon and has been denied it.

At Mr. Loftus's bidding they went slowly to meet the others.

'Doll,' said Mr. Loftus, lingering behind as Peggy and Sibyl walked on together, 'give me your arm. I feel ill.'

'Won't she have me?' said Doll, biting his lip.

'No, my poor boy, she won't.'

CHAPTER II.

'But we are tired.   At Life's crude hands
We ask no gift she understands;
But kneel to him she hates to crave
The absolution of the grave.'

MATHILDE BLIND.

THE laws of attraction remain a mystery. Their results we see.   Glimpses of their workings can occasionally be caught in their broken fragments.   But the curve by which the circle may be drawn is nowhere to be found among those fragments. The first cause we cannot see.   With sacrilegious hands we may rend the veil of its temple in the sacred name of truth, but we shall find nothing in its holy of holies save the bloodstains of generations of sacrifices on its empty altar, and the place where the ark has been.

Youth, beauty, wit—all these attract; but they are only the momentary disciples of a great master, and their power is from him. In his name they perform a few works, and cast out a few small devils.

But now and again a nature appears in our midst in the presence of which youth sinks its voice, and beauty pales and hangs its head, and wit bends its knee in reverence.

What talisman had Mr. Loftus brought into the world with him that disinterested love and devotion should with one exception have followed him all the days of his life? But whether it had been given to him at his birth, or he had found it alone upon the hillside, or Sorrow, who has many treasures in her lap, but will never give them to those who turn from her, gave it to him when he kissed her hand —however this may have been, he had it.

He had gone through his difficult life little realizing how much he owed to the impersonal love and respect which he inspired in men and women, as a beautiful woman seldom realizes how life has been coloured for her by the colour of her hair and eyes.

His poetic exalted nature, with its tender affections, its deep passions, with its refinement and its delicacy of feeling, too sensitive to bear contact with this rough world, and yet not content to dwell apart from awkward fellow-creatures who wounded when they touched it, had leaned twice on the frail reed of personal love, and twice it had pierced his hand. After the second time he withdrew his scarred hand in silence, and journeyed on with it in his bosom.

In the days of his youth he had been swept into the vortex of a deep passion which for the time engulfed his whole being. His early marriage and his romantic love, and his young wife's desertion of him, consumed like a rolling prairie-fire his early life. But he had emerged with the mark of fire upon him, and had taken up life again, and had made a career for himself in the world of politics.

And he had reached middle age, he was a grave man with gray in his hair, before love came to him the second time. How he fared the second time no man knew; but afterwards the love of woman, deep-rooted though it was, died down in Mr. Loftus's heart. He went quietly on his way, but the way wearied him. He confided in no one, for he was burdened with many confidences, and those on whom others lean can seldom find a hand to lean on in their greater weakness and their deeper troubles.

But his physical health wavered. At last his heart became affected, and after a few warnings he was obliged to give up public life. He ceased to be in authority, but he remained an authority, and so lived patiently on from year to year on the verge of the grave, aware that at any moment the next step might be across its brink.

He had spoken the bare truth to Sibyl when he told her that his life hung by a thread. That this is so with all human life is a truism to which we all agree, but which none of us believe. But in his case the sword of Damocles was visible in the air above him. He never took for granted, if he went out for a walk, that he should return; and on this particular May afternoon, as he looked out from a friend's house in Park Lane across the street to the twinkle of green and the coloured bands of hyacinths beyond the railings, he locked his writing-table drawer from force of long habit, and burned the letters he had just read as carefully as if he were going on a long journey, instead of a short stroll across the park to Lady Pierpoint's house in Kensington.

It was a heavy trouble that he had just locked into the writing - table drawer— nothing less than the sale of Wilderleigh, which he and Doll, after much laying together of the gray head and the brown one, had both come to the conclusion could not be staved off any longer. For the newly-imposed death-duties and the increasing pressure of taxation on land, in the teeth of increasing agricultural depression, had been the death-blow of Wilderleigh, as of so many other quiet country homes and their owners. The new aristocracy of the ironmaster and the cheesemonger and the brewer had come to the birth, and the old must give way before the power of their money. Mr. Loftus accepted the inevitable, and Wilderleigh was to be sold.

He did not know for certain where Lady Pierpoint was to be found, but he would try the little house in Kensington. He had seen her driving alone the previous day, and he knew that she had quite recently returned with her daughter and niece from Egypt, where they had spent the winter months. Something in the glimpse of her passing face yesterday had awakened in him a vague suspicion that she was in trouble. She looked older and grayer, and why was she alone?

He took up his hat and, entering the Park, struck across the grass in the direction of the Albert Memorial, blinking in all its gilt in the afternoon sun. The blent green and gray of a May day in London had translated the prose of the Park into poetry. Here in the very heart of the vast machine, Spring had ventured to alight for a moment, undisturbed by the distant roar of dusty struggling life all round her. The new leaves on the smoke-black branches of the trees were for a moment green as those unfolding in country lanes. Smoke-black among the silvery grass men lay strewn in the sunshine, looking like cast-off rags flung down, outworn by humanity, whose great pulse was throbbing so near at hand. Across the tender beauty of the young year fell the shadow of crime and exhaustion, and 'the every-day tragedy of the cheapness of man.'

The shadow fell on Mr. Loftus's mind, and he had well-nigh reached Lady Pierpoint's door before his thoughts returned to her and to her niece, Sibyl Carruthers.

' Pretty, delicate, impulsive creature, so generous, so ignorant, so full of the ephemeral enthusiasms of youth which have no staying power. The real enthusiasms of life are made of sterner stuff than she, poor child! guesses. What will become of her ? What man in the future

will take her ardent, fragile devotion, and
hold it without breaking it, and bask in the
green springtide of her love without dese-
crating it, like those poor outcasts in the
Park?'

Lady Pierpoint was at home, and he was
presently ushered into the drawing-room,
where she was sitting in her walking
things. The room was without flowers,
without books, without any of the small
landmarks of occupation. It had evidently
been arranged only for the briefest stay,
and had as little welcome in it as a narrow
mind.

Lady Pierpoint, pouring tea out of a
metal teapot into an enormous teacup,
looked also as if she were on the point of
departure.

She greeted him cordially, and sent for
another cup. A further glance showed

him that she looked worn and harassed. Her cheerful motherly face was beginning to droop like a mastiff's at the corners of the mouth, in the manner in which anxiety cruelly writes itself on plump middle-aged faces.

'I am not really visible,' she said, smiling, as she handed him the large cup which matched her own. 'I cannot bring forth butter in a lordly dish, as you perceive, for everything is locked up. I am here only for two days, cook-hunting.'

Mr. Loftus had intended to ask after Sibyl, but he asked after Peggy instead.

'She is quite well,' said Lady Pierpoint. 'She is always well, I am thankful to say. I have another Peggy coming out this year—Molly—perhaps you remember her; but how to bring her to London this season I don't know. I have hardly seen anything of her all last winter, poor child! as I was in Egypt with Sibyl. I have only just returned to England.'

'And Miss Carruthers?' he said, examining his metal teaspoon ; 'will not she be in London with you this season, with your own daughters?'

'No,' said Lady Pierpoint, looking narrowly at him ; 'Sibyl is ill. I have been very anxious about her all the winter. I greatly fear that she will sink into a decline. You know, her sister died of consumption a year or two ago.'

Mr. Loftus looked blankly at Lady Pierpoint.

'Sibyl!' he said—'ill? Oh, surely there is some mistake? What do the doctors say?'

'They all say the same thing,' said Lady Pierpoint, her lips quivering. 'She had a cough last winter, and she is naturally delicate, but there is no actual disease as yet. But if she continues in this morbid state of health—if she goes on as she is at present—they say it will end in that.'

Mr. Loftus was silent.

Lady Pierpoint looked at his unconscious, saddened, world-weary face, and clasped her hands tightly together.

'Mr. Loftus,' she said, 'I am going to put a great strain on our friendship, and if I lose it, I must lose it. I have been thinking of writing to you, but I could not. I had thought of asking you to come and see me while I was alone here, but my courage failed me. But now that you have come by what is called chance, I dare not be a coward any longer. Sibyl has told me of what passed last summer between you and her.'

A faint colour came into Mr. Loftus's pale face. He kept his eyes on the floor.

' I think,' he said gently, but with a touch of reserve in his voice which did not escape his companion, ' we must both forget that as completely as she herself has probably already forgotten it.'

' She has not forgotten it,' said Lady Pierpoint, ignoring, though with a pang, his evident wish to dismiss the subject. ' It is that which is causing her ill-health. She can think of nothing else. Some of us,' she said sadly, ' are so constituted that we can bear trouble and disappointment— others can't. This poor child, who has cried for the moon, is not mentally and physically strong enough to bear the disappointment of being denied it. And the doctors say that her life is dependent on her happiness.'

Mr. Loftus rose, and paced up and down the room. She dared not look at him.

Presently he stopped, and, with his face turned away, said with emotion :

'But the moon is a dreary place if it is seen as it is, with its extinct volcanoes and its ice-fields. Nothing lives there. The fire in it is burnt out, and there is snow over the ashes. It is only in the eyes of a child that the moon is bright. We elders know that it is dark and desolate.'

Lady Pierpoint was awed. She had known Mr. Loftus for twenty years. He had been kind to her in the early years of her widowhood, and in the later ones had helped on her boys by his influence in high quarters. She had often told him of her difficulties, but she had never till now heard him speak of himself.

Her great admiration for him, which was of a humbler kind than Sibyl's, led her to say : 'It is not only in the child's eyes that the moon is bright.'

She might have added with truth that in her own middle-aged eyes it was bright, too.

'I greatly honoured you when Sibyl told me about it,' she continued, after a long pause. 'It is because I have entire trust in you that I have told you the truth about this poor child, who is as dear to me as my own, though I hope my own will face life more bravely. Should you, after reflection, feel able to do her this—this— great kindness, I hope you will come and stay with us at Abergower for Whitsuntide. But—I shall not expect you, and I shall not mention to anyone that I have asked you.'

She rose and held out her hand. She looked tired.

He held it a moment, and she endeavoured to read the grave, inscrutable glance that met hers, but she could not.

'Thank you,' he said, and went away.

'How dare she think of him?' said Lady Pierpoint to herself.

CHAPTER III.

'L'amour est une source naïve, partie de son lit de cresson, de fleurs, de gravier, qui, rivière, qui, fleuve, change de nature et d'aspect à chaque flot.'— DE BALZAC.

IN England Spring is a poem. In the Highlands of Scotland she has the intensity of a passion. The crags and steeps are possessed by her ; they stand transfigured like a stern man in the eyes of his bride. And here in these solemn depths and lonely heights, as nowhere else, shy Spring abandons herself, secure in the fastnesses where her every freak is loved. She sets the broom ablaze among

4—2

the gray rocks, yellow along the river's edge, yet hardly yellower than the leaves on the young oak just above. The larches hear her voice, and hundred by hundred peep over each other's heads upon the hillside, all a-tremble with fairy green. The shoots of the dwarf cherry, scattered wide upon the uplands, are pink among the grass. The primroses are everywhere, though it is Whitsuntide—behind the stones, among the broom, beside the little tumbling streams, in every crevice, and on every foothold. The mountain-ash holds its white blossoms aloft in its careful spreading fingers. Even the silver birch forgets its sadness while spring reigns in Scotland.

There are those to whom she speaks of love, but there are many more to whom she whispers, 'Be comforted.' When hope leaves us, it is well to go out into the woods and listen to what Spring has to say. Though life is gray, the primroses are coming up all the same, and the young shafts of the bluebell pierce the soft earth in spite of our heartache. A hedge-sparrow has built him a house in the nearest tangle of white hawthorn. There will be children's voices in it presently. Be comforted. Hope is gone, but not lost. You shall meet her again in the faces of the children, God's other primroses. She is not lost. She has only taken her hand out of yours. Be comforted.

But Sibyl refused to be comforted. Her love for Mr. Loftus, if small things may be called by large names, was the first violent emotion of a feeble and impulsive mind in a feeble body, both swayed by veering influences, both shaken by the changing currents of early womanhood, as a silver birch is shaken with its leaves.

A woman with a deeper heart, and with a slight perception of Mr. Loftus's character, would have reverently folded her devotion in her heart and have gone on her way ennobled by it. But with Sibyl, to admire anything was to wish to possess it; to tire of anything was to cast it away.

Mr. Loftus was in her eyes without an equal in the world. Therefore—the reasoning from her point of view was conclusive—she must marry him. She had no knowledge, she had not even a glimpse, of the gulf of feeling, far wider than the gulf of years, which separated him from her. She imagined no one appreciated him, or entered into the dark places of his mind, as she did. She mistook his patient comprehension of her trivial aspirations, and his unfailing kindness to all young and crude ideas, for the perfect sympathy of two kindred souls, and was wont to speak mysteriously to Peggy of how minds that were really related drew each other out and enriched each other.

It is always a dangerous experiment to awaken a sleeping soul to the pageant of life. Mr. Loftus had endeavoured to do this for Sibyl, consciously, gently, with great care, out of the mixed admiration and pity with which she inspired him, in the hope that, in later years, when her feet would be swept from under her, she might find something to cling to, amid the wreck of happiness which his dispassionate gaze foresaw that she would one day achieve out of her life.

He had run the risk which all who would fain help others must be content to run— the risk that their work will be thrown away. He saw that the little rock-pool which reflected his own face was shallow, but he had not gauged the measure of its shallowness. His deep enthusiasms, tried and tempered before she was born, weary now with his own weariness, aroused hers as the Atlantic wave, sweeping up the rocks, just reaches and arouses the rock-pool, and sends a flight of ripples over it, which, if you look very close, break in mimic waves against the further edge. And before the thunder of the wave is silent the pool is glass once more.

On natures like these the only influence which can make any impression is a personal one. It is overwhelming while it lasts ; but it is the teacher who is every--

thing—the teaching is nothing. And when he is removed, they passively drift under another personal influence, as under another wave, and the work of the first, the foundation patiently and lovingly built in its pretty yellow sand, is swept away, or remains in futile fragments, as a mark of the folly of one who built on sand.

Certain strong, abiding principles Mr. Loftus had sought to instil into Sibyl's mind. She had perceived their truth and beauty; but she cared nothing for them in reality, and had fallen at the feet of the man who had awakened those exquisite feelings in her.

And now either she would not, or could not, get up. She clung to her imaginary passion with all the obstinacy which is inherent in weak natures. The disappointment had undermined her delicately-poised

health.   As she walked down towards the
Spey alone on this particular June afternoon, she looked more fragile and ethereal
than ever.   The faint colour had gone
from her cheek, and with it half her evanescent prettiness had departed.   Her slight,
willowy figure seemed to have no substance
beneath the many folds of white material
in which her despairing dressmaker had
draped her.   With the suicidal recklessness
of youth, she made no attempt to turn her
mind to other thoughts, but pondered
instead upon her trouble, with the un-
reasoning rebellion against it with which,
in early life, we all meet these friends in
disguise.

She picked her way down the steep
hillside, through the wakened broom and
sleeping heather, and along the edge of
the little oasis of oatfield, where so many

thousands of round, river-worn stones had been gleaned into heaps, and where so many thousands still remained among the springing corn. The long labour and the patience and the partial failure which that little field meant, reclaimed from the heather, but not wholly reclaimed from the stones, had often touched Lady Pierpoint, who knew what labour was ; but it did not appeal to Sibyl.

She sat down with a sigh on the river-bank, a forlorn white blot against the crowded world of green, with Crack, her little Scotch terrier, beside her, and looked listlessly across the sliding water, which ran deep and brown as Crack's brown eyes, and loitered shallow and yellow as a yellow sapphire among its clean gray stones and gleaming rocks. A pair of oyster-catchers sped upstream, low over the water, swift as eye could follow, with glad cries, like disembodied spirits that have found wings at last and feel the first rapture of proving them.

' Happy birds !' said Sibyl to herself. ' They do not know what trouble means.'

Crack, who had heard this sentiment, or something very like it, before, stretched himself methodically, both front-legs together first, and then the hind-legs one by one, and walked slowly down to the edge of the water and sniffed sadly, as one who knows that search is vain among the stones for a rat which is not there. Crack had a fixed melancholy which nothing could dispel. His early life had been passed in the activity of a camp, and his spirit seemed to have been permanently embittered by the close contemplation of military character. He had been round

the world. He knew the principal smells
of our Eastern empire, but no reminiscences
of his many travels served to brighten the
gloomy tenor of his thoughts. He was
sad, disillusioned, still apt to hurry and
shorten himself through doors, and to
retreat under sofas to brood over imaginary
wrongs. All games distressed him. He
went indoors at once when the red ball
was produced which transformed Peter
from an elegant poodle into a bounding
demon. But in spite of his melancholy
he was liked. He went out but little, but
where he went he was welcomed. He
was a gentleman and a man of the world.
No dog ever quarrelled with him. He met
bristling overtures with a mournful tact
which turned growls into waggings of
tails. He himself was seldom seen to wag
his tail, except in his sleep.

He returned from the water's edge and sat down on an outlying fold of Sibyl's gown.

In the sunny stillness a wild-duck, with cautious, advanced neck, and a little fleet of water-babies, paddled past, bobbing on the amber shallows. Crack raised his ears and watched them. His feelings were so entirely under control that he could scratch himself while observing an object of interest ; and he did so now. But he did not move from his seat on Sibyl's gown. He was disillusioned about wild-ducks, who did not play fair and stick to one element, but would take to their wings when hard pressed in the water, like a woman who changes her ground when cornered in argument.

Presently the afternoon sun shifted, and all the larches on the steep hillside opposite

and all the broom along the bank stooped
to gaze at a flickering fairyland of broom
and larches in the wide water. The deep
valley of the river was drowned in light.
Only the bank on which Sibyl was sitting
under the mountain-ash had fallen suddenly
into shadow.

'Like my life,' she thought, and rose
to go.

Who was this coming slowly towards
her along the little path by the water's
edge?

She stood still, trembling, her hands
pressed against her breast.

It was he. It was Mr. Loftus. He
was looking for her. He was coming to
her. Joy and terror seized her.

He saw her standing motionless in her
white gown under the white blossom-laden
tree. And as he drew near and took her

nerveless hands in silence, and looked into her face, he saw again in her deep eyes the shy, imploring glance which had met him once before—the mute entreaty of love to be suffered to live.

'Sibyl,' he said, and in his voice there was reverence as well as tenderness—reverence for her untarnished youth, and tenderness for the white flower of love which it had put forth, 'will you be my wife?'

CHAPTER IV.

'J'ai vu sous le soleil tomber bien d'autres choses
Que les feuilles des bois et l'écume des eaux,
Bien d'autres s'en aller que le parfum des roses
Et le chant des oiseaux.'

ALFRED DE MUSSET.

'Mummy,' said Peggy, a few days later, coming into her mother's sitting-room and pressing her round, cool cheek against Lady Pierpoint's, ' why does Sibyl want to marry Mr. Loftus ?'

' Because she thinks she loves him, Peggy, as many other women have done before her.'

' I think I love him, too, in a way,' said

5

Peggy. 'He is better than anybody. When I am with him, I feel—I don't know what I feel, only I know it's good, and I want to do something for him, or make him something really pretty for his handkerchiefs ; but—I don't want to marry him.'

'That is as well, my treasure, as he is going to marry Sibyl.'

'I never thought he would marry anybody. I can't believe it. It seems as if it could not happen.'

'It will happen,' said Lady Pierpoint, 'if he lives.'

'Sibyl says,' continued Peggy, 'that he enters into her feelings as no one else does, and that she understands him, and that hardly anyone else does except her, because he is so superior.'

'Indeed !'

'And she says she can speak to him of aspirations and things that she can't even mention to Molly and me. She says it isn't our fault—it is only because we are different to her.'

'You are certainly very different,' said Lady Pierpoint, compressing her lips.

'And to think that she might have married Mr. Doll,' continued Peggy, as if Sibyl's actions were indeed inscrutable. 'Mr. Doll will be twenty-eight next August. He was twenty-seven when we were at Wilderleigh last year. If I had been Sibyl, I would have married him, and then I'll tell you, mummy, what I would have done. I would have asked Mr. Loftus to let us live with him at Wilder-leigh, and I would have taken such care of him—oh! such care—and I would have spent whole bags of money on the farms and fences and things, and he would have been happy, and Mr. Doll would have been happy, too.'

'Peggy,' said Lady Pierpoint, 'shall I tell you a secret? I think that is exactly what Mr. Loftus hoped Sibyl would do.'

Mr. Loftus returned to London a day or two later, and had an interview with Doll the day before the announcement of the engagement appeared in the *Morning Post*.

Mr. Loftus was attached to his nephew —people always looked upon Doll as his nephew, though he was in reality his first cousin—and to him and to him alone he told the circumstances which had led to his engagement.

What passed between the elder man and the young one during that interview will never be known. But when at last Mr. Loftus left him, Doll sat for a long time looking over the geraniums into the park. The somewhat dull, unimaginative soul that dwelt behind his handsome expressionless face was vaguely stirred.

'It's a mistake,' he said at last, half aloud. 'But Uncle George is on the square ; he always is.'

And when he was ruthlessly twitted next day by his brother officers on being cut out by his uncle, he replied simply enough :

'He is a better man than me, as all you fellows know. She would not have looked at one of you any more than she would at me. I suppose she had a fancy for marrying a man who could spell, which none of us can.'

'Spelling or none,' said the youngest

sub—'which is an indecent subject which should never be mentioned between gentlemen—anyhow, I mean to borrow a thousand or a fiver off him. Mr. Loftus always tipped me at school.'

One of Mr. Loftus's first actions was to stop the preliminary proceedings regarding the sale of Wilderleigh, which he had been arranging a month ago, on the afternoon when he had called on Lady Pierpoint. It was like awakening from a nightmare to realize that Wilderleigh would not be sold, after all. He almost wished that he might live long enough to set the place in order for Doll.

The engagement was a nine days' wonder, and those nine days were purposely spent by Mr. Loftus in London. He was aware that many cruel things would be said at his expense, and that

the bare fact that a man of his years and
in his state of health should marry a young
heiress, and so great an heiress as Sibyl
Carruthers, must call forth unfavourable
comments. People who did not know
him said it was perfectly shameful, and
that it was just the sort of thing which
those people who posed as being so extra'
good always did. How shocked Mr.
Loftus had pretended to be when old
Lord Bugbear, after his infamous life,
married a girl of seventeen! And now
he, Mr. Loftus, was doing exactly the
same himself. Of course he had a very
fascinating manner—just the kind of
manner to impose on a young girl who,
like Miss Carruthers, knew nothing of
the world, and had been nowhere. And
everyone knew he was desperately poor.
Wilderleigh could hardly pay its way. A

rumour had long been afloat that it would
shortly be for sale. If he had not been so
hard up for money it would have been
different; but it was a most disgraceful
thing, and Lady Pierpoint ought to be
ashamed of having exposed the poor
motherless girl left in her charge to his
designs upon her. They wondered how
much Lady Pierpoint, whose means were
narrow, had been bought over for. The
sums varied according to the sordidness
of the different speculators, who of course
named their own price.

Others who knew Mr. Loftus were
puzzled and were silent. To know him
at all was to believe him to be incapable
of an ignoble action; yet this marriage
had the appearance of being ignoble—
not, perhaps, for another man, but certainly
for him. His intimate friends were dis-

tressed, and greeted him with grave cordiality and affection, and hoped for an explanation. He gave none. And they remembered that never in his public or in his private life had he been known to give an explanation of his conduct, and came to the conclusion that they must trust him.

Mr. Loftus had recognised early in life that explanations explain nothing. If those who had had opportunities of knowing him well misjudged him after those opportunities, they were at liberty to do so as far as he was concerned. The weight of an enormous acquaintance oppressed him, and, though he had never been known to wound anyone by withdrawing from an unequal friendship, which he had not been the one to begin, and which was an effort to him to continue, still, he took advantage of being misunderstood to lay aside many such friendships. It was not pride which prompted this line of action on Mr. Loftus's part, though many put it down to pride, especially those who had held aloof from him at a certain doubtful moment, and in whose regard subsequent events had entirely reinstated him, and who complained that he expected to be considered infallible. It was, in reality, the natural inclination of a world-weary man of the world to lay aside, as far as he could courteously do so, the claims of the artificial side of life, its vain forms, its empty hospitalities.

He realized that for the purpose of winnowing its friendships the various events of life may be relied on to furnish the fitting occasions. Those who do not wish to offend others by leaving them need make no effort, for they will certainly be presently deserted by those who have never grasped the meaning of the character which has been the object of their transient admiration. 'If he is unequal he will presently pass away.' Mr. Loftus neither hurried the unequal, self-constituted friend, nor sought to detain him. But when he departed, shaking the dust from off his feet, the door was noiselessly closed behind him, and his knock, however loud, was not heard when he returned again.

A small batch of uneasy admirers left him on the occasion of his engagement. They said openly that they were much disappointed in him, and that he had shaken their belief in human nature.

'Will Sibyl also pass away?' Mr. Loftus wondered, as he sat on the terrace at Wilderleigh on his return from London. 'Yes, she, too, will presently pass away; but I shall not give her time to do so. She will be absorbed by her first love for a few years, and I shall only remain a few years at longest. By the time it wanes I shall be gone, and my departure will pain her but very slightly.'

His face softened as he thought of Sibyl. His nature, which, in its far-away youth, had been imaginative and romantic, had remained sympathetic. He gauged, as few others could have done had they been the object of it, the measure of her romantic attachment to himself. It was perhaps safer in his hands than in those of a younger man. For youth perpetrates many murders and mutilations in the name of love, as the schoolboy's love of a butterfly finds expression in a pin and a cork. But it would have cut Sibyl to the heart if she had even guessed that his tranquil mind took for granted that her adoration would not last until the stars fell from heaven and the earth fell into the sun. For 'Les esprits faibles ne sont jamais sincères.' That is a hard saying, but alas! and alas! that it is only the weak who believe that it is not true. The strong know better, but if they are merciful they are silent.

'And so my second wife is also to be an *esprit faible*,' said Mr. Loftus to himself, looking at the past through half-closed eyes. 'But in the meanwhile I have learnt a lesson in natural history. I shall not expect my butterfly to hew wood and draw water. And this time I shall not break my heart because pretty wings are made to flutter with.'

And the remembrance slid through his mind of Millais's picture of the dying cavalier, and the butterfly perched upon the drawn sword in the ardent sunshine. And he thought of the drawn sword of Damocles hanging over his own life, and Sibyl's love preening itself for one brief second upon it. And at the thought he smiled.

CHAPTER V.

'Je suis l'amante, dit-elle.
Cueillez la branche de houx.'
VICTOR HUGO.

'When all the world like some vast tidal wave with-
draws.'—BUCHANAN.

MANY persons prophesied that the marriage
between Mr. Loftus and Sibyl would not
take place, but it did.

On a burning day late in July they were
married in London, for Sibyl's country
place, where Mr. Loftus had hoped the
wedding might have taken place, was
shut up.

Lady Pierpoint did all in her power to

make the wedding a quiet one, for his sake. Very few invitations were sent out, and there was no reception afterwards. But, nevertheless, though the season was at its last gasp, when the day came the un- fashionable London church was crammed with that 'smart' world, half of which had condemned Mr. Loftus, while it showered invitations upon him.

Many hundreds of eyes were fixed upon his stately feeble figure as he moved slowly forward to place himself beside the young girl, whose emotion was plainly visible, and whose bouquet shook in her hand. The contrast between the two, as they stood together, was of that glaring description which appeals to the vulgar and conventional mind, on which shades of difference are lost.

Mr. Loftus went through the ceremony

with equanimity. His grave face betrayed nothing except fatigue and the fact that he was suffering from a severe headache. Lady Pierpoint and Doll watched him with anxiety, while Peggy, standing close behind the bride, wept silently, she knew not why.

'Oh, mummy,' she said afterwards when it was all over, and Sibyl, anxious, preoccupied, had left Lady Pierpoint and Peggy and Molly, who had been mother and sisters to her, without a tear, without a regret, without a backward look, absorbed in the one fact that Mr. Loftus was ill—'oh, mummy, you say Sibyl loves him so much. Is that why she did not mind going away from all of us a bit? I know he had a headache, but she never used to mind when you had a headache, and when she was ill, do you remember how she

6

always sent for you, even when I told her
you were resting? And yet she used to
be a little fond of us. But since he came
she does not seem to care for us any more.
If one loves anybody, does one forget the
others?'

'Some women do,' said Lady Pierpoint,
taking Peggy's red, tear-stained face in
her hands and kissing it. She could not
bear to own, even to Peggy, how wounded
her warm maternal heart had been because
Sibyl, whose delicacy had given her so
many anxious hours, had shown no feeling
at parting with her. Mr. Loftus had
shown much more, when he had come to
speak to her alone for a few minutes in
her sitting-room, when the carriage was at
the door.

'Some women,' said Lady Pierpoint,
looking wistfully at her daughter, 'forget

everyone else when they marry, and are very proud of it. They think it shows how devoted they are. A little cup is soon full, Peggy, and a shallow heart, if it takes in a new love, has no room left for the old ones. The new love is like the cuckoo in the nest—it elbows out everything else.'

'I will not be like that,' said Peggy, crushing her mother and her mother's bonnet in an impulsive embrace. 'I will have a deep, deep heart, mummy, and no one shall ever go out that once comes in —and—oh, mummy, you shall have the best bedroom in my heart always!'

'I have a very foolish girl for a daughter,' said Lady Pierpoint, somewhat comforted, smiling through her tears, 'and one who has no respect for my best bonnet.'

*   *   *   *   *

At Sibyl's wish she and Mr. Loftus went straight to Wilderleigh. They reached it after several hours' journey on the evening of their wedding-day. And gradually the nervous exhaustion and acute headache from which he had been suffering, and which had become almost unbearable in the train, relaxed their hold upon him. They were sitting in the cool, scented twilight on the terrace. Through the half-darkness came the low voice of the river talking to itself. Noise and light and other voices, and this dreadful day, were gone at last.

He gave a sigh of relief and smiled deprecatingly at her. They had hardly spoken since they were married. She was sitting near him, a slender figure in her pale gown, that shimmered in the feeble light. But there was light enough for her to see him smile, and she smiled back at him with her whole heart in her lovely eyes. No thought of self lurked in those clear depths, and Mr. Loftus, looking into them, and remembering how, on this her wedding day, her whole mind had been absorbed, to the entire oblivion of a bride's divided feelings, in the one fact that he was suffering, was touched, but not with elation.

The long listless hand lying palm upwards on his knee made a slight movement, and in instant response to it her hand was placed in his. His closed over it. Perhaps nothing could have endeared her more to him than the mute response that had waited on his mute appeal, and had not forestalled it.

His hand clasping hers, he drew her slightly, and, obeying its pressure, she leaned towards him.

'My Sibyl!' he said, and she involuntarily drew closer to him, for something in his voice and manner, in spite of their exceeding gentleness and tenderness, seemed to remove him from her. ' Fate has been hard upon you that I should have been ill on your wedding-day.'

' No,' she said, timidly pushing off from shore into the new world upon her little raft. ' Fate was kind, because to-day has been the first day when I could be with you and take care of you.'

' You take too much care of me.'

' I care for nothing else,' she said, her voice faltering, adoration in her eyes.

One white star peered low in the western heaven through the violet dusk.

' Once long ago, before you were born,' said Mr. Loftus, ' I loved someone, and she said she loved me, and we were married. But after a time she brought trouble upon me, Sibyl.'

The great current had caught the little raft, and was hurrying it out to sea.

'I will never bring trouble upon you,' said the young girl, her lips trembling as she stooped to kiss his hand. 'When you are tired you shall lean on my arm. When your eyes are tired I will read to you. I will take care of you, and keep all trouble from you.'

'Till I die,' he said below his breath, more to himself than to her.

'Till you die,' she answered.

And so, but this time very lightly, Mr. Loftus leaned once again, or made as if he leaned, on the fragile reed of human love.

CHAPTER VI.

'He has nae mair sense o' humour than an owl,
and a' aye haud that a man withoot humour sudna
be allowed intae a poopit.'—IAN MACLAREN.

THE arrival of Sibyl at Wilderleigh was
the occasion of many anxious surmises at
the little Vicarage on the part of the young
Vicar and his young and adoring wife.

It had long been a great grief to them
that Mr. Loftus only came to church once
on Sunday. It was vaguely understood
that he had yielded himself to doubts on
religious subjects, which alone could account for this 'laxity'—doubts which the

young Vicar felt could not have shaken himself or Mrs. Gresley, and which he was convinced he could dispel. But he could never obtain an opportunity to wage war against these ghostly enemies, for though he had preached during Lent a course of sermons calculated to pulverize the infidel tendencies of the age, which his wife had pronounced to be all-conclusive and to place the whole affair in a nutshell—it certainly did that—unfortunately the person for whose spiritual needs they were concocted did not hear them.

Mr. Gresley had several times called upon Mr. Loftus with a view to giving the conversation a deeper turn, but when he was actually in his presence, and Mr. Loftus's steel-gray attentive eye was upon him, the younger man found it difficult, not to say impossible, to force conversation on subjects which Mr. Loftus had no intention to discuss.

'If he would only meet me in fair argument!' Mr. Gresley said on his return from a futile attempt to approach Mr. Loftus on the subject of public worship ; ' but when I had thoroughly explained my own views on the importance of regular attendance at both services on Sunday, he only said that those being my opinions, he considered that I was fully justified in having daily services as well. If he would only meet me fairly and hear reason,' said the young clergyman ; ' but he won't. The other day when I pressed him on the subject of the devil—I know he is lax on the devil—I said : " But, Mr. Loftus, do you not believe in him ?" If he had only owned what I am sure was the case— namely, that he did not believe in him—

I could have confuted him in a moment.
I was quite ready. But he slipped out of
it by saying, " Believe in him ! I would
not trust him for a moment." There is no
arguing with a man who scoffs or is silent.'

' My dear,' said Mrs. Gresley, ' infidels
are all like that, and their only refuge is to
be silent or profane. Don't you remember
when that professor from Oxford, whom
we met at Dr. Pearson's, said something
about history and the Bible—I forget
what, but it was perfectly unorthodox—
and Dr. Pearson was so interested, and
you spoke up at once, and he made no
reply whatever, and then asked me the
name of our Virginia creeper, and talked
about flowers. I often think of that, and
how he had to turn the subject.'

' But he was not convinced,' said Mr.
Gresley, frowning ; ' that is the odd part of

it. He brought out a book on the Bible
with things in it much worse than what he
said in my presence, and which I positively
refuted. And it went through six editions,
and the Bishop actually read it.'

'You see,' said Mrs. Gresley, with the
acumen which pervades the atmosphere of
so many country vicarages, 'a man like
the professor does not *want* to be convinced, or his books would not be read,
any more than Mr. Loftus wants to be
convinced he ought to come to church
regularly, because then he would have no
excuse for staying away. But perhaps his
wife may be a Christian, James. They
say she is quite a young girl, and that her
aunt has brought her up well.'

And when Sibyl's sweet face and black
velvet hat, and a wonderful flowing gown
of white and lilac, appeared in the carved

Wilderleigh pew beside Mr. Loftus's
familiar profile, the Gresleys hoped many
things; though Mrs. Gresley expressed
herself, after service, as much shocked at
the bride's style of dress, which she pronounced to be too showy. Mrs. Gresley's
views on dress were exclusively formed at
the two garden-parties and the one private
ball to which she went in the course of the
year. The Gresleys thought it wrong to
go to public balls, and—which was quite
another matter—they thought it wrong for
other clergymen and their wives to go also.

It was fortunate that Mr. Loftus admired his wife's style of dress, as he had
always admired Sibyl herself, from her
graceful, fringeless head to her slender,
low - heeled shoes. She pleased his
fastidious taste as perhaps no other woman
could have done. She was one of the few

Englishwomen who can wear French gowns as if they are part of them, and not put on for the occasion.

After a becoming interval Mr. and Mrs. Gresley called, and this time Mrs. Gresley was somewhat mollified by what she called the very ' suitable ' costume of brown holland in which Sibyl received them. Mr. Loftus did not appear, and in the course of conversation the young couple were further pleasantly impressed with the perfect orthodoxy and sound Church teaching of the bride, whose natural gift of platitude was enhanced by the subject under discussion.

They also made the discovery that Mr. Loftus was, in his wife's opinion, infallible. And Mrs. Gresley looked with some astonishment at a bride who actually entertained towards a ' layman ' the unique sentiments which she did for her apostolic James.

'She is a nice young creature,' said Mrs. Gresley, half an hour later, as, with her hands full of orchids, she accompanied her lord back to the Vicarage, 'and her views, James, are beautiful—just what I think myself. She agreed with everything we said. She must have been very well brought up. · But I can't understand her infatuation for Mr. Loftus. Really, from the way she spoke of him, and how he knew best, one might have supposed he was priest as well as squire here. It almost made one smile.'

Mr. Loftus and Crack had, in the meanwhile, remained in the gardens, he leaning back in a long deck-chair, looking dreamily up into the perspective of moving green above him, while Crack, who had only just arrived from Scotland, snapped mournfully at the English flies, which tasted very much the same as those of Strathspey, so few new things are there under the sun.

Sibyl had wished to bring Peter, the poodle, also to Wilderleigh, but nothing would induce Mr. Loftus to invite him. He told Sibyl that he himself hoped to replace Peter in her affections, and he had certainly succeeded.

She returned to him now, and sat down on a low stool at his feet. In these early days she was much addicted to footstools and the lowest of seats, provided they were properly placed. They were in harmony with her sentiments, and facilitated an upward gaze.

'They were so pleasant. I wish you had come in,' she said.

'I find the clergy as fatiguing as Anderson's beetle found cleanliness,' said Mr. Loftus, his eyes dwelling on her. 'But that is not their fault. It is because I happen to be a beetle.'

'I was a little tired, too,' said Sibyl hastily. 'They stayed rather long.'

'And did you like them?'

'Yes; I thought them very nice. And I am glad they are High Church. I think it is so much nicer, don't you?'

'Do you mean to tell me, now that we are married and it is too late to go back, that you are High Church?'

'Oh, not very high!' said Sibyl anxiously, yet reassured by his look of amusement. 'Which are you?'

'I am the same as Mr. Gresley,' said Mr. Loftus slowly, 'with a difference.'

'I thought you were different,' said

7

Sibyl, gratified at her own powers of observation.

'I know,' continued Mr. Loftus, 'that he thinks I have no principles at all, because he believes they are not the same as his; but in reality they are very much the same as his, only they are carried further afield, and he loses sight of them, while he has a neat little ring-fence round his own. I like Mr. Gresley very much. He is an exemplary young man. But some people become very narrow by walking in the narrow path, and I fear he is one of them. Remember this, my Sibyl, that there is no barrier in your own character against which someone, sooner or later, will not stumble to his hurt. No boundary in ourselves will serve to shut God in, as this good young man thinks, but every boundary will at last shut out some fellow-creature from us, and be to one, whom perhaps we might have helped, an occasion of stumbling. And now let us show Crack the brook. I am afraid he will think but little of it after the Spey, but he will be too polite to say so. As he only arrived yesterday, it is premature to put it into words, but I have an intuition that Crack and I shall become friends. If I had any influence over him, I would encourage him to bathe in the brook, for he brought into the house with him this morning an odour that convinced me that we were on the eve of some great chemical discovery.'

So they wandered down by the brook, across the lengthening shadows. A cock pheasant was clearing his throat in the wood near the gardens. The low sun had become entangled in the rookery. A pair of sandpipers were balancing their slender selves on a tiny beach of sand. A little black and white water-ousel darted upstream with rapid, bee-like flight. Crack followed, gravely investigating the bank point by point, as if on the look-out for some fallacy in it.

And Sibyl registered the conclusion in her own mind that one must be 'wide,' like Mr. Loftus, not narrow, like Mr. Gresley. After this conversation she always spoke of her religious convictions as 'wide.'

CHAPTER VII.

'We form not our affections. It is they
    That do form us; and form us in despite
Of our poor protests.'
                                    LYTTON.

SUMMER slid into autumn, and autumn into winter. The first few months of married life had been difficult to Mr. Loftus, but he had brought his whole attention and an infinite patience to bear on them, and gradually his reward came to him. Sibyl could learn because she loved. She learned slowly, but still she did learn, to read, not her husband's thoughts— those were far from her—but his wishes. She discovered, with a pang which cost

her many secret tears—but still she did
discover—that he often wished to be alone,
and that she must not go into his study
unless she were asked to do so.   She
learned gradually when to join him when
he paced in the rose-garden, and when it
vexed and wearied him to have her 'by
him.   And she learned, too, after the first
horrible experience, which neither could
remember without anguish, when, with
blue lips, he had begged her not to
touch him ; that when he had an attack
of the heart she must not betray her agony
of mind, if she was to be allowed to remain
in the room, and she must not ignorantly
try to apply the remedies, but must leave
it to Mr. Loftus's valet, whose imperturb-
able calm and promptitude had often
ministered to his master before.   Sibyl's
terror of death and violent emotion at

its approach were peculiarly trying to
Mr. Loftus, who had long since ceased
to regard death with horror, and only
wished to be allowed to meet it quietly,
without a scene.

All intimacy was difficult to his solitary
nature. It was alien while it was courteously welcomed. It was the natural
instinct of hers. She had to learn to
suppress her tenderness—or, at any rate,
its expression—a hard lesson for an over-
demonstrative nature, not long out of its
teens. But Sibyl learned even that for
his sake. And there her knowledge
stopped. It never reached beyond his
wishes to his mind. She was merged
entirely in her love of her husband, but
if he had been unworthy of the exalted
pedestal on which she had placed him,
she would not have discovered it.

'It might just as well have been Doll,' Mr. Loftus thought occasionally, half amused, when he had the barbarity to try a platitude of the first water upon her— one of Doll's best, such as the young man, after diving into the recesses of his being, could produce, and found she received it with as much interest as the thoughts for which he had dug deep. For hero-worship was necessary to Sibyl, but not a hero— only that she should consider him one. The sham was to her the same as the real. She saw no difference. Like many another woman, she would have adored an ass's ears, wondering at the blindness of the rest of mankind. But if the truth about those ears had been forced upon her, rubbed into her, tattooed upon her, her entire belief in human nature would have fallen with the fall of one fellow-creature. The heights and depths of human nature had never awed her, nor its great forces moved her to reverence or compassion. She was of the stuff out of which the female cynic, as well as the female devotee, is made.

Mr. Loftus did not marvel at an adora‐ tion which has been the birthright of his fortunate sex since the world began, but his perennial wonder at the enigma of feminine human nature had a new element added to it—that of amusement. She played with his tools, as a robin perches on a spade, thinking it is stuck in the earth for that purpose, and for the turning up of worms.

The struggles, the despair, the hope and the aspiration, through which his youth had climbed, and out of which it had forged its tools, were not a part of Sibyl's youth. She liked the tools now that they were made, and desired them for her own small uses. She was naturally drawn to those of deeper convictions and larger faiths. She liked the luxury of being moved by them, stirred by them, lifted beyond herself by a power outside of herself. She loved to nibble the edge of their hard-earned bread and feel that she, too, was of them, and make believe that she had helped to grind the flour ; and to make believe with Sibyl was the same thing as to believe. Her insolvent nature clung to the rich one, ostensibly because it was sympathetic, but really because it was rich.

This unconscious audacity was a novel source of entertainment to Mr. Loftus, a bubbling wayside spring which he had hardly hoped to meet with on the dry highroad of married life. It is greatly to be feared that his conscience, usually a tender one, was hardly as watchful as it should have been on this subject. It certainly had lapses when Sibyl conversed with him seriously, especially when she coupled his feelings with her own on the greatest subjects, never doubting that they were identical. But after a short time he dared not speak to her of anything really dear to him. She had a gift for making sacred things common by touching them, and age had not tarnished reverence in Mr. Loftus's soul, though it had tarnished many things which youth holds in reverence. He talked to her, instead, on subjects which he had not much at heart, and that did quite as well.

And she, on her side, would bring to him the inferior religious books, and superficial unorthodox works which she believed to be deep because they were unorthodox, which were the natural food of her little soul, and he received them and her remarks upon them, as he received a flower when she gave him one, with courtesy and gratitude.

So absorbed was she in her devotion to her husband, and in the interchange of beautiful sentiments, that her other duties, increased by her position at Wilderleigh, were not even perceived. Unobservant persons are sometimes surprised at the real devotion — and Sibyl's was real —of which a shallow and cold-hearted nature shows itself capable. But those who look closer perceive at what heavy expense to others that one link is held, which is in reality only a new and more subtle form of selfishness.

She dropped the other links without even knowing that she had dropped them.

She had no tender, watchful gratitude for
Lady Pierpoint, no interest in Peggy's new
gowns and lovers, or as to whether Molly
had enjoyed her first season. If this had
been pointed out to her, she would have
glibly ascribed the result to marriage,
which, according to some women, is the
death-bed of all sympathy and impersonal
love. It is like ascribing sin to tempta-
tion.

The Gresleys were much disappointed
in her, and they had reason to be so, for
Sibyl had changed over after her discovery
of Mr. Loftus's convictions, or, rather, her
interpretation of them, and, instead of being
rather High Church, had now decided to
be 'wide,' which state, it soon appeared,
was not compatible with being an efficient
helper to the earnest hard-working young
couple at her gate. Mr. Loftus, who now

had command of money, was far more considerate than his wife.

'She,' Mrs. Gresley complained, 'did not seem to care to do anything with her life, for she would neither sing in the choir nor teach in the Sunday-school.'

She did consent to give prizes for needlework in the schools, but when the day came it was discovered that she had forgotten all about it, and, as she had a cold, Mr. Loftus drove into the nearest town and brought a mind weighted with political matter to bear upon the requisite number of prizes suited to girls of from seven to fourteen years, and hurried back just in time to prevent disappointment by distributing them himself.

'Have you written lately to Lady Pierpoint?' he sometimes asked, and Sibyl generally had to confess, 'Not lately,' and then she would write and then forget again.

'I suppose Lady Pierpoint is less well off now that you are married?' he asked one day tentatively. 'No doubt your guardians made her an allowance while you lived with her.'

'Yes,' said Sibyl, who was sitting on the hearthrug, trying to make Crack do his trick of sitting up. It was his only trick, and he could not do that unless he happened to be sitting down when called upon to perform it. If he were on all fours at the moment, he could not remember how it began. 'Aunt Marion often said it was a very handsome allowance.'

'And have you continued it, or part of it?' asked Mr. Loftus gravely.

Sibyl owned that she had never thought of doing so.

'Everything I have is yours now,' she said, looking up at him.

'And I am spending it,' he said, 'freely. Thousands of yours are being put into the estate, in repairs, and new farms and buildings. I am like the man in Scripture who pulled down his barns to build greater —at least, who intended to do so if he had had time.'

Mr. Loftus stopped. For the first time for many years a faint wish crossed his mind that his soul might not be required of him till all those expensive improvements were paid for, which would make Doll's position as landlord easier than his own had been.

'Even in these bad times,' he went on, 'Wilderleigh will come round. You have taken a great weight off my mind, Sibyl.'

'That is what I wish,' she said, turning

her face, as he put back a little ring of hair behind her ear, so that her lips met his hand.

'But Lady Pierpoint? I am afraid, Sibyl, her husband left her very badly off.'

' I will write now,' said Sibyl, springing to her feet.

Crack rose too, and jumped on Mr. Loftus's knees, quietly pushing his hands off them with his strong nose, and accommodating his long, thin body by a few jerks into the groove which a masculine lap presents. Mr. Loftus did not want him, and it tired him to keep his knees together ; but he knew there was a draught on the floor, and he allowed him to remain.

' How much shall I say ? A thousand a year or fifteen hundred for her life?' asked Sibyl, dipping her pen in the ink. It was all one to her. She always gave

8

freely of what cost her nothing—namely, money.

'It must not be too much, or she won't feel able to take it,' said Mr. Loftus, considering. 'And if it is an annuity, it does not help the children.' And he wondered how far he dared go.

And when, a few days later, Lady Pierpoint received a note from Sibyl, very delicately and affectionately expressed, and offering, in such a manner as to make refusal almost impossible, a sum of money more than sufficient to provide for both her daughters, she guessed immediately whose tact had. dictated the letter.

'Sibyl would never have thought of it,' she said to herself, as she wrote a note of acceptance. 'It never crossed her mind when she left us, or even to offer to pay for Peggy's and Molly's bridesmaids' gowns, although she chose such expensive ones. And if it had occurred to her since, she would not have put it like that.'

CHAPTER VIII.

'Le monde est plein de gens qui ne sont pas plus sages.'—LA FONTAINE.

WITH the winter came many invitations, but they were nearly all refused, for Mr. Loftus had long since dispensed himself from attending county festivities, and Sibyl, though she had recovered her health, was always delicate. Lady Pierpoint had had doubts as to whether she ought to winter in England, but not only was Sibyl herself determined so to do, but when Lady Pierpoint saw her in London before Christmas with a vivid colour and an elasticity of bearing which made a marked contrast to the drooping, listless demeanour of the previous winter, her doubts were at once set at rest.

Presently, however, an invitation came for a masked ball in the immediate neighbourhood, which Mr. Loftus decided could not be refused.

'But why should we go?' said Sibyl, 'if we don't care about it. And I hate balls, and I hate society. I was saying so to the Gresleys only yesterday. I love my own fireside and a book.'

Sibyl had no idea how much these occasional mild flourishes, which found great favour at the Vicarage, annoyed Mr. Loftus. She put them forth, poor thing! with a view to showing him how much she had in common with him.

'It is a mistake to say you hate society,'

said Mr. Loftus, ' because you are not in a position to hate what you have never seen. Personally, I can see nothing peculiarly obnoxious in my fellow-creatures when they have their diamonds and white ties on. I do not even discover that they are more worldly in ball-gowns than on other occasions.'

' But it is all so empty and vain,' said Sibyl; 'and though I dare say I have not seen much, still, the small-talk is so wearying, and I suppose that is the same everywhere. I should not mind society if there was any real conversation, anything *deep.*'

Sibyl loved the word ' deep.' She used it on the occasions when others use the word 'trite,' she meaning the same as they did, but looking at the trite from a different angle. From her point of vantage, eccentricity was originality, and a wholesale contradiction of established facts a new view.

Mr. Loftus was so close on the verge of annoyance that he was obliged to be amused instead.

'I have heard many people say they hated society,' he said, smiling, and Sibyl smiled back at him, delighted at having won his approbation by the nobility and originality of her sentiments.

'I have generally found that they are persons to whom, probably for some excellent reason, society has shown the cold shoulder, or those, like the Gresleys, who have never seen anything of it, and who call garden-parties, and flower-shows, and bazaars, and all those dismal local functions, society.'

'She is not going to this masked ball,'

said Sibyl. 'I asked her, and she said, "Of course not. Her husband being a clergyman made it quite impossible." I wonder why she always says things are quite impossible for the clergy that most of the other clergy do. She said the same about the Hunt Ball.'

'That was because of the pink coats of the men and the new gowns of the women, and also partly because they were not asked. It happened to be a good ball, consequently it was dangerous. Dowdiness has from a very early date of this world's history been regarded as a sacrifice acceptable to the Deity, so naturally pretty gowns and electric light are considered to be the perquisites of the Evil One.'

'But are we really going to this ball?'

'We are. It would be unneighbourly

not to do so. I met Lady Pontesbury yesterday in D——, and she begged us to support her, and to bring even numbers. People cannot give balls in the country, Sibyl, if none of the neighbours will take the trouble to fill their houses. I have seen very cruel things of that kind done. Ours is the largest house in the neighbourhood, and, as it now has a mistress, we must fill it.'

The idea of society having any claim on her was a new light to Sibyl. She had always considered herself superior to its blandishments. But now that she discovered that Mr. Loftus actually regarded certain social acts as a duty, and this masked ball as one in particular, she immediately changed her opinion, and forthwith looked upon it as a duty also. It was a duty which, as its fulfilment drew near, became less and less unpleasant to anticipate.

She had until now lent a sympathetic ear to the Gresleys when they talked of society as a snare, and had echoed Mr. Gresley's remarks on the same.

'Balls are not wrong in themselves,' Mr. Gresley would say in his chest voice, keeping his hand in before Sibyl and his admiring wife. 'It is only the abuse of them that is blameworthy. Use the world as not abusing it. A carpet dance among young people I should be the last to blame. We cannot keep the bow always at full stretch. But when it comes to ball after ball, party after party, and pleasure is made a business, instead of a recreation, by which I mean that which restores elasticity to the exhausted faculties, re-creates us in fact, and renews our energy

for our work, then indeed——' And Mr.
Gresley would express himself at that
length which is apparently the one great
compensation of the teacher who has no
pupils.

Sibyl enjoyed his conversation very
much. She thought Mr. Gresley a very
sensible person, and his opinions were in
harmony with her own.

Mrs. Gresley had also declared, after a
brief visit to Kensington in July during
the 'sales,' that she had neither the means
nor the inclination to throw herself into
the social whirlpool which she and Mr.
Gresley had dispassionately viewed from
two green chairs in the Row, and which
Mr. Gresley had estimated 'at its true
worth.' If she had possessed both the
means and the inclination, she would
perhaps have discovered that she was no

nearer to that vortex than the many thousands who annually make a pilgrimage to London only to be tossed on the outermost ripple of the whirlpool, and who revolve for ever on the rim of society like Saturn's rings, without approaching the central luminary. But that it is difficult to be loved of Society and ensnared by her the Gresleys and Sibyl did not know, any more than that certain crimes require great qualities in order to commit them.

Mr. Loftus might have been able to relieve their ignorance, but, as Sibyl told the Gresleys, he did not care much for conversation.

A habit of silence was certainly growing upon him since his marriage.

CHAPTER IX.

'Et chacun croit fort aisément,
  Ce qu'il craint.'
                    LA FONTAINE.

THE night of the masked ball had arrived.
A large party had assembled at Wilderleigh, including Lady Pierpoint and her
daughters, and Doll. It was Doll's first
visit to Wilderleigh since Mr. Loftus's
marriage, and as he looked down the
dinner-table at Sibyl he wondered at his
own folly in coming. He thought he had
'got over it,' but to-night he found that
he had made a sufficiently grave mistake
in supposing so. Unimaginative persons

never know when they have got over anything, because they have no fore-knowledge in absence of the stab which a certain presence can inflict. So Doll walked stolidly in—where Mr. Loftus in a remote but not forgotten passage of his own life had feared to tread—and then writhed and bit his lip at the hurt he had inflicted upon himself.

In the days when he had hoped to marry Sibyl, he had often pictured her to himself —his imagination could reach as far as tangible objects, such as furniture and food and raiment—sitting at the head of his table, talking to his guests, wearing the Wilderleigh diamonds, and looking as she looked now; for to-night Sibyl was beautiful. And it had all come about, except one thing—that she was married to Mr. Loftus instead of to him. He turned to look fixedly at Mr. Loftus talking to Lady Pierpoint, and saw as in some new and arid light his thin stooping figure in the carved high-backed chair, the refined profile with the high thin nose and scant brushed-back gray hair, and the bloodless Vandyke hand holding his wine-glass. Mr. Loftus had a very beautiful hand. Doll had not seen Mr. Loftus and Sibyl together except at the altar-rails. And as he looked rage took him. It was a monstrous marriage. The blood rushed to his face, and beat in his temples. And a sudden bitter hatred surged up within him against Mr. Loftus as man against man. He looked at him again in his gray hair and his feebleness, and loathed him.

And Mr. Loftus's indifferent kindly glance met his, and he smiled quietly at him. And the cold fit came after the hot one, and poor Doll cursed himself, and told himself for the first time of many times— of how many times!—that the greatest evil that could befall him in life would be to become estranged from ' Uncle George.'.

' What are you thinking of?' said Peggy's voice at his elbow. Peggy was often at Doll's elbow at other times besides dinner, a fact which did not escape Lady Pierpoint's maternal eye, but for which she did not reprimand Peggy, any more than for her slightly upturned nose and little upper lip, which turned up in sympathy too. But Peggy vaguely felt that on this occasion her dear ' mummy ' was rather in the way, especially when the whole party assembled in the hall in their masks and dominoes, and Peggy could not sufficiently admire Doll's flame-coloured garment with a black devil outlined on the back and a hood with pointed ears. She had no eyes for Captain Charrington, the tallest man in the Guards, magnificent in crimson silk from head to foot, with crimson mask as well, or for another of Doll's companions in arms in a chessboard domino of black and white with an appalling white mask.

'Look, Peggy,' said Lady Pierpoint, 'at Mrs. Devereux. I think I have never seen any domino as pretty as her white one with little silver bees all over it.'

Mrs. Devereux protested, in a muffled manner, through the lace edge of her mask that Miss Pierpoint's and Mrs. Loftus's duplicate primrose ones edged with gold quite put her bees into the shade.

'Into a hive you mean,' said her husband, a dull young man in dove colour.

9

'But how are we to know Mrs. Loftus and Miss Pierpoint apart?'

'You won't know us,' said Sibyl; 'that is just the point.'

*   *   *   *   *

'There is one thing I ought to have asked you before,' said Sibyl solemnly in her married-woman voice, as the brougham in which she and Mr. Loftus had driven together drew up in the *queue*.   'Would you like me to dance or not?'

'Are you fond of dancing?'

'Very—at least, I mean I don't mind.'

'Then, dance by all means.'

'You are quite sure it is what you wish. I thought perhaps as a married woman——'

'Married goose,' said Mr. Loftus, laughing, perfectly aware that she would have liked him to be jealous.

*   *   *   *   *

'I'm going to dance,' whispered Sibyl to Peggy, as they followed Mr. Loftus and Lady Pierpoint, the only unmasked ones of the party, towards the ballroom. 'He says he wishes me to. He is always so unselfish.'

But Peggy's open eyes and mouth and whole attention were turned to the ball-room which they were entering.

Lord and Lady Pontesbury were standing near the entrance solemnly shaking hands with the masked hooded figures who came silently towards them. No introductions were possible. Lord Pontesbury almost embraced Mr. Loftus, so relieved was he to see a human face. Lady Pontesbury beamed on Lady Pierpoint.

'Your girls here?' she whispered. No one seemed able to speak above a whisper.

'Yes,' said Lady Pierpoint below her

breath, looking helplessly round at the twenty muffled figures in her wake. And Captain Charrington came forward at once, and said he was the eldest, and produced Doll as his youngest sister, while Peggy and Molly wondered how anyone could be so funny and live.

The long ballroom, with its cedar-panelled walls outlined in gilding, was brilliantly lighted. The floor of pale polished oak shone like the pale walls. Banks of orchids rose in the bay-windows. In the brilliant light a vast crowd of spectral figures stalked about in silence, clad in every variety and incongruous mixture of colour.

'Like devils out on a holiday,' said a voice from the depths of a fool's cap and bells.

Mr. Loftus was at once surrounded by

masked figures who shook hands with him warmly. A Bishop was the centre of another group, ruefully responding to he knew not whom, half the young men in the room telling him that they had met him last at the Palace when they were ordained.

One mischievous couple were making the circuit of the room, conversing with the chaperons one after the other, who smiled helplessly at them and answered but little, for middle-aged ladies with daughters out have other things to think of besides repartee. Captain Charrington sustained his character of a wit by walking about growling at intervals in a mysterious and interesting manner.

The band took its courage in both hands, and broke the silence. A tremor passed through the crowd. There was a momentary pause, a momentary uncertainty as to the sex of the hooded figures, and then forty, fifty, seventy couples of demons were solemnly polkaing.

Mr. Loftus smiled. Sibyl, standing by him, laughed till he gently urged her to take it more quietly. Lord and Lady Pontesbury turned for a moment from the fresh arrivals, and their mournful faces relaxed. The Bishop, who seldom saw anything more enlivening than a confirmation or a diocesan gathering, shed tears. The trombone collapsed, the wind instruments wavered, and left the violins for a moment to make desperate music by themselves. Then the band pulled itself together, and the music and the flying feet rushed headlong on.

※   ※   ※   ※   ※

Doll, who had hardly spoken to Sibyl that day, came up to claim his dance.

'I can't dance any more,' she said plaintively. 'My domino weighs me down. Let us sit out.'

'Shall we go into the gallery,' said Doll, 'and watch the unmasking from there? It is a quarter to twelve now, and every one unmasks at twelve.'

He did not know whether to be glad or sorry that she would not dance with him. 'Better not,' he said to himself. But he had thought of the possibility of that dance many times before he reached the ballroom, and had decided that it was his duty to ask her.

They left the ballroom, and, passing numerous ghostly figures sitting in nooks and on the wide staircase, they made their way to the arched gallery which overhung the ballroom. Every white arch had been lit by a pendent pink-shaded lamp, and the arches and Sibyl's primrose domino all took the same rosy hue. In nearly every arch a couple were already sitting, watching the crowd below. Doll secured one of the few vacant places, and Sibyl drew her chair forward and leaned her slender bare arms on the white stone balustrade. The couple in the adjoining archway were chattering volubly, but Doll and Sibyl did not talk. She did not notice the omission, for her eyes were following the quaint pageant with the delight of a child. Doll racked his brains for something to say, and found nothing.

Why had she married Uncle George? Why had she married Uncle George? So, as he could not ask her that, and tell her that he cared for her a hundred times more than her husband did, he said nothing.

The *pas de quatre* was in full swing. The men, annoyed by their long dominoes, and having one hand disengaged, raised their voluminous skirts and danced with long black legs, regardless of propriety. Captain Charrington's endless crimson domino had come open in front and displayed his high action to great advantage. A very elegant pink domino, which had been introduced by the eldest son of the house as an heiress to all the men whom he did not recognise, and which had danced only with masculine dominoes, was now seen to emulate its partner, and to have black trousers rolled up above its white-stockinged ankles, and rather large white satin shoes.

'Look!' said the girl in the next archway; 'that pink domino must be Mr. Lumley. He often acts as a woman.'

'Hang him for an impostor! I've danced with him as such,' said the man, with ill-concealed vexation. 'He knew me, and called me by name. I took him for——' He did not finish his sentence. 'By Jove! that black domino with a death's-head and cross-bones is a good idea,' he went on. 'Is it half-mourning, do you suppose?'

'How foolish you are! That is Lord Lutwyche. I have just been dancing with him.'

'Lord Lutwyche is not here. He sprained his ankle at hockey yesterday.'

The female domino appeared to be a prey to uneasy reflections.

'The primrose domino is the prettiest in the room,' she said presently. 'And

how well she dances! I wonder who
she is.'

' I happen to know that is Mrs. Loftus.'

Sibyl, with her back to the arch, could
hear every word on the other side of it.
Doll was not near enough. This was
indeed delightful! How lucky that she
and Peggy had come dressed alike!

' Which is Mr. Loftus?' said the
woman's voice eagerly. ' I have heard
so much about him.'

' That tall, thin, fine-looking old chap
with his hands behind his back, standing
by the Bishop. The Union Jack domino
is speaking to him.'

' So that is he. I have always wished
to see him. He looks tired to death.

' He always looks like that. Quite a
character, though, isn't he?'

' He has an interesting face. But it

was a disgraceful thing, his marrying a
pretty young girl, and an heiress, at his
age.'

Sibyl made a sudden movement, and
the other couple glanced round. They
saw her, but her primrose domino had
taken the pink of her surroundings, and
they suspected nothing.

'I'm not so sure. His nephew stands
up for him, though his uncle cut him out,
and his nephew ought to know. I fancy
there was more in that marriage than
outsiders suspect. I've heard it said more
than once that she fell head-over-ears in
love with him, and he married her out of
pity.'

The last words fell distinctly on Sibyl's
ears, and at that second the music ceased
with a crash, and a gong boomed out,
engulfing all other sounds. It was twelve

o'clock. A bell somewhere just above them was counting out twelve slow strokes, just too late—just ten seconds too late.

She leaned back sick and shivering.

She did not realize that the crash and the tolling bell were part of the evening's programme. They seemed to her the natural result of the words she had just heard. If she had been crossed in love at Lisbon before the earthquake, she would have regarded that upheaval as the immediate consequence of her lacerated feelings.

'Look, look!' said the woman; 'they are unmasking.'

A confused sound of laughter and surprise and recognition, and a widespread hum of conversation, came up to them.

Everyone was streaming out of the gallery, and in the ballroom there was a vast turmoil, as of hiving bees, and a throng at every door.

'Shall I take you to the cloak-room to leave your mask and domino?' said Doll, turning to her at last, from watching without seeing it what was passing below. He took off his velvet mask as he spoke. The sullen wretchedness of his face fitted ill with the pointed rakish ears which still surmounted it.

She did not answer. He saw that the outstretched hand still on the balustrade was tightly clenched.

'Mrs. Loftus,' he said. 'Sibyl! what is it? Are you ill?'

She tore off her mask, and, as if she were suffocating, plucked with trembling hands at the gold ribbon that fastened her hood and domino.

He was alarmed, and clumsily helped

her to loosen them. Her small face,
released from the mask, looked shrunk
and pinched like a squirrel's in its thrown-
back hood. The pink glow upon it from
the lamp was in horrible contrast with
its agonized expression.

'What is it? what is it?' said Doll, in
distress nearly as great as her own, taking
her little clenched hand, and holding it, still
clenched, in his large grasp. 'Are you ill?'

She shook her head impatiently.

'Would you like—shall I—fetch Mr.
Loftus?'

She winced as if she had been struck.

'No,' she gasped; 'I will not see him—
I will not see him!'

A change came over Doll's face. Involuntarily, his hand tightened its clasp on
hers.

* * * * *

'These entertainments,' said the Bishop to Mr. Loftus, as they paused for a moment in the gallery, and looked down into the ballroom, which was now rapidly refilling with gaily-dressed women and pink and black coats, 'are, I believe, typical of English country life.   They are—ahem! —the gallery seems conducive to conversation; it is, in fact, a—er—whispering-gallery.'   Here he turned, smiling, to Mr. Loftus.   'Perhaps Mr. Doll has hardly reached the stage at which he will call upon me to officiate—just so; we will go down by the other staircase—but I trust, though I might be in the way at present, that my services may be required a little later on.'

'I should like to see Doll married,' said Mr. Loftus, who had been not a little surprised at the eager manner in which the young man was bending towards the figure with her back towards them, whose fallen-back hood intercepted her features. He recognised the domino.

'I had no idea Peggy had made such an impression,' he said to himself.

As he re-entered the ballroom, he met Lady Pierpoint, also returning to it with her two plump little girls in tow, whom she had been tidying in the cloak-room. Captain Charrington and some of the other men from Wilderleigh were waiting near the doorway, claiming first dances as their party came in. The orchestra, who had been refreshing themselves, were re-mounting to their places.

'Then, where is Sibyl?' said Mr. Loftus, looking at Peggy.

'She went to the gallery a long time ago,' replied Peggy promptly, 'with Mr.

Doll, to see the people unmask at twelve o'clock.'

Mr. Loftus smiled. 'It was a horrible sight as seen from below,' he said; 'half the men's faces were black, and the hair of every one of them stood up at the back.'

The band struck up a swaying, languorous valse such as tears the hearts out of young persons in their teens.

*   *   *   *   *

'I must go home,' Sibyl kept repeating feverishly. 'Doll, you must get the carriage. I must go home.'

Doll was engaged to Peggy for this valse, but he had forgotten it. Sibyl was engaged to Captain Charrington, but she had forgotten it.

He was terrified, as only reticent persons can be, lest her loss of self-control should be observed. He helped her to her feet, and took her to the cloak-room, she clinging convulsively to him. Her entire disregard of appearances filled him with apprehension. The cloak-room was empty, even of attendants, for it had been thronged till within the last ten minutes, and now the wave had surged back to the ballroom, and the maids, their duties finished, had slipped away to see the spectacle.

Sibyl cast herself down on a chair, shivering. Her little Grecian crown of diamonds fell crooked.

'Let me fetch Lady Pierpoint,' said Doll urgently.

'No, no,' she said imploringly; 'I want to go home. Oh, Doll, get the carriage, and take me home. Is it so much to ask?'

He looked at her in doubt. She was not fit to return to the ballroom. Evidently she would make no attempt to conceal her despair, whatever its cause might be, from the first chance comer.

'I will take you,' he said; and he rushed out to the stables, found the Wilderleigh coachman, and himself helped to put the horses into the brougham.

'It was ordered for one o'clock especially for Mr. Loftus,' said the coachman, hesitating, 'and the landau, and the fly, and the homnibus for half-past three.'

'You will be back in time for Mr. Loftus,' said Doll. 'Mrs. Loftus is ill, and must go home immediately.'

He had the brougham at the door in ten minutes, and returned to the cloakroom to find a maid standing by Sibyl with a glass of water. Sibyl was still shivering, holding on to the chair with both hands, her eyes half closed, her face ghastly.

'I am afraid the lady is ill,' said the servant.

It was very evident that she was ill.

'The carriage is here,' said Doll. 'Can you manage to walk to it?'

She rose unsteadily, and the maid wrapped her in her white cloak. It annoyed Doll that the maid evidently looked upon them as an interesting young married couple.

He gave Sibyl his arm, and she staggered against him. He hesitated, and then compressed his lips, put his arm round her, and, half carrying, half leading her, helped her to the carriage.

It was a white night with snow upon the ground. The band was playing one

of Chevalier's songs.   Out into the solemn
night came the urgent appeal of ''Enery
'Awkins' to his Eliza not to die an old
maid, accompanied by the dull, threshing
sound of many feet.

As the carriage began to move, Sibyl
seemed to revive, and a moan broke from
her.

'Oh, Doll,' she said suddenly, turning
towards him and catching his hand and
wringing it. 'It isn't true, is it?   It is
only a horrible lie.'

'What isn't true?' he said fiercely, almost
hating her for the pain she was causing
him, not his hand.

'It isn't true what that man said in the
next arch, that—that Mr. Loftus married
me out of pity?'   And she swayed herself
to and fro.

She had asked the only person to whom

Mr. Loftus had confided his real reasons for his marriage.

It had been on the tip of Doll's tongue all the evening to say: 'Why did you marry him? *I* would have married you for love.' But he mastered himself.

'It isn't true, is it?' gasped Sibyl.

Doll set his teeth.

'No,' he said. 'It's a lie. He married you for love. He—*told me so!*'

CHAPTER X.

'Pour connaître il faut savoir ignorer.'—AMIEL.

'DOLL,' said Mr. Loftus, the morning after the ball, when all the guests had departed, except the Pierpoints, 'I do not expect absolute perfection in my fellow-creatures, but it appeared to me that you fell rather below your usual near approach to it last night. What do *you* think ?'

Doll answered nothing.

'You see,' went on Mr. Loftus, 'after twelve o'clock, when everyone unmasked, was the time when I should naturally have introduced Sibyl to many of our friends.

and neighbours, as this was her first public appearance since her marriage, and I could not do so on our arrival. The fact that she had left the house without me, and—without my knowledge—was unfortunate.'

It had been more than unfortunate in reality. Mr. Loftus, whose marriage had made a great sensation in his own county, had been begged on all sides, as soon as the masks were off, to introduce his wife, and, though he had not shown any surprise at her non-appearance and Doll's, he had at last been obliged to retire to the men's cloak-room and wait there till his carriage came, so as to obscure the fact that she had departed without him. He had been annoyed at what he took to be Doll's heedlessness of appearances.

'She felt ill, and wished to go home,'

said Doll, reddening, and not perceiving that he was offering an explanation which did not cover the ground. He would have been perfectly satisfied with it himself.

'I greatly fear that she *is* ill,' said Mr. Loftus; 'but she was quite well when she went to the ball last night. She is very delicate and excitable. Is it possible that anything occurred to upset her ?'

Mr. Loftus fixed his keen steel-gray eyes on Doll. He had seen, as he saw everything, Doll's momentary jealousy of him the evening before.

For the life of him Doll could not think what to say. It seemed impossible to tell Mr. Loftus the truth, and he had but little of that inventive talent which envious persons with a small vocabulary call lying. That little had been used up the night before. Yet, perhaps, if he had been aware that Mr. Loftus had seen him with Sibyl in the gallery in an attitude which allowed of but few interpretations, his slow mind might have grasped the nettly fact that he must explain.

Mr. Loftus waited.

'My boy,' he said at last, 'I am not only Sibyl's husband'—he saw Doll wince —'but I am also, I verily believe, her best friend.'

There was no answer.

A slight, almost imperceptible, change came over Mr. Loftus's face. He paused a moment, and then went on quietly :

'Sibyl is most generous about money— too generous. I am almost afraid of taking an unfair advantage of it, though she presses me to do so. But I am pushing on the repairs everywhere ; and I am rebuilding Greenfields and Springlands from the ground. They will get to work again directly the frost is over. I have the plans here, if you would like to look at them.'

He drew a roll out of the writing-table drawer, and spread it on the table. Doll perceived with intense relief that the subject was dropped, and he knew Mr. Loftus well enough to be certain that it would never under any circumstances be reopened. But as he looked at the plans, and Mr. Loftus pointed out the new well and the various advantages of the designs, it dawned upon Doll's consciousness that he was losing something which he had always regarded as a secure possession, and which nothing could replace — Mr. Loftus's confidence.

He had seen it withdrawn in this gentle

fashion from other people, who did not find out for years afterwards that it was irrevocably gone. And he became aware that he could not bear to lose it.

'Here,' said Mr. Loftus, putting on silver-rimmed pince-nez, 'is, or ought to be, the new private road leading out on to the H—— highroad. I decided to make it, Doll, not only for the convenience of the farm, but also because I cannot let that row of cottages with any certainty until there is an easier means of access to them. My father always intended to make a road there. I only hope,' he said at last, letting the map fly back into a roll, 'that I shall live to pay for all I am doing, but I can't pay for unfinished contracts. If I don't, Doll, you will have to raise a mortgage on the property to pay for the actual improvements on it. Sibyl has left all her fortune to me, I believe; but as I am certain to go first, Wilderleigh will not be the gainer.'

And it passed through Mr. Loftus's mind for the first time that perhaps, after all, Sibyl might still marry Doll some day. How he had once wished for that marriage he remembered with a sigh.

'It may be. Youth turns to youth,' said Mr. Loftus to himself, as he went up to his wife's room after Doll had left.

Sibyl was ill. A chill, or a shock, or excitement—who shall say which?—had just touched the delicate balance of her health and overset it. It toppled over suddenly without warning, without any of the preliminary struggles by which a strong constitution or a strong will staves off the advance of illness. She gave way entirely and at once, and the night after the night of the ball it would have been difficult to recognise, in the sunk, colour-less face and motionless figure, the brilliant, lovely young girl in her little diamond crown.

Sibyl's illness did not prove dangerous, but it was long. Lady Pierpoint, who had nursed her before, sent her daughters home, and took her place again by the bedside, with the infinite patience which she had learned in helping her husband down the valley towards the death which at last became the one goal of all their longing, and which had receded before them with every toiling step towards it, till they had both wept together because he could not, could not die. Perhaps it was because her husband had gone through the slow mill of consumption that Lady Pierpoint's heart had so much tenderness for Sibyl, for whom only a year ago she had dreaded the same fate.

Mr. Loftus had the nervous horror of, and repugnance to, every form of illness which as often accompanies a refined and sympathetic nature as it does an obtuse and selfish one. And his lonely existence had not brought him into contact with that inevitable side of domestic life. He was extraordinarily ignorant about it, and his natural impulse was to avoid it.

But he stood by his wife's bedside, adjusted his pince-nez, and accepted the situation. For many days Sibyl would take nothing unless given it by himself, would rouse herself for no voice but his. Lady Pierpoint marvelled to see him come into Sibyl's room at night in his long gray dressing-gown, to administer the food or medicine which the nurse put into his hand. His patience and his kindness did not flag, but it seemed to Lady Pierpoint as if at this eleventh hour they should not have been demanded of him; and it wounded her—why, it would be hard to say—to watch him do for Sibyl with painstaking care the little things which in her own youth her young husband had done for her, the little things which in wedded life are the great things.

Mr. Loftus sometimes made a mistake, and once he forgot that he was married, and was found pacing in the rose-garden oblivious of everything except a political crisis—but only once. He was faithful in that which is least.

Lady Pierpoint felt with a twinge of conscience that when she had endeavoured to bring about this marriage she had been selfishly engrossed in Sibyl's welfare.   She had not thought enough of his.

And gradually Sibyl recovered, and went about the house again, wan and feeble, and Lady Pierpoint left Wilderleigh.

CHAPTER XI.

*' Dark is the world to thee ? Thyself art the reason
why.'*

TENNYSON.

CONVALESCENCE is often accompanied by a
depression of spirits rarely experienced
during the illness itself. A weak nature
seeks for a cause for this depression in its
surroundings, and when it finds one, as it
invariably does, it hugs it. These causes,
thanks to the assiduity of one whom we
are given to understand has seen better
days, are seldom far to seek; and it
requires a very strong will to hold fast
the conviction that these paroxysms of de-

11—2

pression arise from physical weakness, and not from some secret woe. Sibyl had not a very strong will. After the first novelty of convalescence was past, and she had been installed in her sitting-room in a cascade of lace and ribbons, which her dressmaker called a *saut du lit*, and after Mr. Loftus had gravitated back towards the library on the ground-floor and his article for the *Millennium*, Sibyl began to experience that vague weariness and distaste of life which all know who know ill health.

It is at this stage that the unprincipled invalid becomes 'the terror of the household and its shame.' It is at this stage that lengths of felt are laid down in passages by tender and injudicious parents, because no sound can be borne by sensitive ears, that the children are 'hushed,' the blinds are drawn down, and doctors who encourage exercise and light are speedily discovered to have misunderstood the delicate constitution with which they have to deal.

If Sibyl had not had a cause for depression, she would most certainly have manufactured one. But unfortunately she had a real one. The incident of the masked ball rankled. Doll had lied. He had done his poor best, but he had not lied well. His eyes had not quite looked her in the face when he told her that Mr. Loftus had married her for love. His voice had not that emphatic ring which the crude mind ever recognises as the ring of truth, and which in consequence the progressive one applies itself to acquire.

Her mind, dulled by illness and narcotics, had half forgotten that she had been momentarily distressed. But now the remembrance came back like a nightmare. The grain of sand, blown by chance into her eye, pricked, and she sedulously rubbed it into an inflammation.

She remembered now that there had been an earlier incident in his courtship which had not been satisfactorily explained, *when he proposed to her the second time.* Sibyl always regarded his offer under the mountain-ash as *the second time.* She had a vague feeling that he had proposed before. She had said as much to one or two friends in confidence. But now that she came to think of it, she remembered that it was she who had proposed *the first time*, and had been refused. This minor detail of an uncomfortable incident had until now almost slipped out of her memory, which, like that of many women whose buoyancy depends on the conviction of the admiration of others, seldom harboured anything likely to prove a worm in that bud.   •

But now she applied to the whole subject that mental friction which morbid minds believe to be reflection, until it became, so to speak, inflamed.

Why had he sworn before the altar and the Bishop to love her, if he did not love her? She became tearful, listless, apathetic. She sat for hours looking into the fire, unemployed, uninterested. The evil spirit which ever lurks in sofas and couches whispered in her ear, when it pressed the cushions, that she was indeed miserable, that her husband avoided her, that she was an unloved martyr, that no one felt for her or sympathized with her. It did not tell her that she had been

married for her money, simply because no
sane person could look at Mr. Loftus and
believe that.   But she changed in manner
towards him.   She was cold, formal.   She
turned away her head when he came into
the room, and then when he had left it
wept in secret because she had been
married out of pity.

And yet in her heart of hearts, if she
had such a thing, had she not partly
guessed that fact long ago, and wilfully
shut her eyes to it?   The chance words
she had overheard were only the confirmation of a latent misgiving.   Does any
woman ever really remain in ignorance if
she is not loved, or if she has been
married for other reasons than love?
What constant props and supports she had
given to Mr. Loftus's love for her!   It
had never been allowed to stand alone.

Why had she from the first always
bolstered it up by continually saying to
herself and others, until she almost believed it: 'My husband is so devoted to
me. My love is such a little thing beside
his. What have I done to deserve such a
great devotion?' How often she had said all
these things that tepidly-loved women say!

Seeming to observe nothing, Mr. Loftus
saw all, and pondered over the reason of
her altered appearance, and her visibly
changed feeling towards himself since the
night of the masked ball. If it were that
her health was threatened as it had been
before her marriage, why should her
affection towards himself have undergone
this change? Could it be anything to do
with Doll? And in these days Sibyl was
more frequently in his thoughts than in the
early days of his marriage with her. The

thought of her came between him and the political article which the editor of the *Millennium* had asked for.

'Time will show,' he would say to himself, with a sigh, taking up his pen again.

One afternoon soon afterwards he came into her sitting-room, and found her in tears.

' Has Crack said anything unkind?' he asked gently, while Crack beat his tail in the depths of the fur rug in courteous recognition of his own name.

' No,' she said, turning her head away.

' Have I, then?' sitting down by her.

' No.'

' Then, my child, what is it?'

' Nothing,' she said faintly.

. There was a pause.

'Is it the same nothing that troubled
you the night of the ball?'

He saw her start and shrink away from
him.

'Oh! did Doll tell you?' she gasped,
turning crimson.

'My dear, he told me nothing,' said Mr.
Loftus gently, moving slightly away from
her, and looking at her with grave attention.
He greatly feared that unhappiness was
before her in some form or other. He
waited in the hope that she would speak
to him of her own accord. But she only
began to cry again. She was still weak.
Was it possible that she was afraid of him?
What could be troubling her that she, who
did not know what reticence meant, could
fear to tell him, which yet Doll knew?
Doll was in love with her. Had he lost
his head on the night of the ball? Had

she discovered that she and Doll were young?

'Crack,' said Mr. Loftus, 'I have a very neglectful wife. I come to ask for something for my headache, and she pays no attention to me at all.'

In earlier days Sibyl would have been on the alert in a moment if Mr. Loftus's sacred head confessed an ache. Now she moved slowly to the writing-table and produced certain innocuous remedies which he had brought to her and asked her to apply for him after that terrible time when he had had an attack of the heart and had repulsed her.

Presently the headache was better, and Mr. Loftus went back to the library and lit his pipe, which was remarkable, because he was as a rule unable to smoke after a headache.

He sat motionless a long time, his eyes fixed.

'I hope,' he said at last, knocking the ashes out of his pipe, 'that I shall not live to become Sibyl's natural enemy, for I think I am about the only real friend she has in the world.'

And the small seed that would have quickened in another man's heart into a deep-rooted jealousy remained upon the surface of his mind as a misgiving, which took the form of anxiety for her.

CHAPTER XII.

'Oui, sans doute, tout meurt; ce monde est un
     grand rêve,
Et le peu de bonheur qui nous vient en chemin,
Nous n'avons pas plus tôt ce roseau dans la main,
Que le vent nous l'enlève.'
                                ALFRED DE MUSSET.

SIBYL continued pale and listless, and
presently Mr. Loftus found fault with her
gowns. They were not new enough. The
colours of her tea-gowns did not suit her.
He suggested that she should go to
London to Lady Pierpoint's house for a
few days to see her dressmaker, and added,
as an afterthought, that he should like her

to consult the specialist to whom she had
gone on former occasions, and whose name
he had reason to remember.

Sibyl received the suggestion of this
visit in silence. She did not oppose herself
to it, but left the room to shed a torrent of
angry tears in private. The truth, which
seldom visited her feeble judgment, did
not tell her that Mr. Loftus was anxious
about her health. Hysteria took up the
tale instead, and officiously informed her
that he was tired of her. He wanted to
get rid of her. Men were always like that
after they had been married a little time.
What was a woman's love and devotion to
them when the first novelty had worn off?
She would go. She would certainly go ;
and when she was gone she would write to
him, telling him that she saw only too
plainly that his love for her was dead,

and that she had decided never to return, and at the same time making over to him her entire fortune, reserving only for herself a pittance, on which she would live in seclusion in a cottage in some remote locality.

She was somewhat consoled as she thought over the dignified, the harrowing letter which she would compose in London. Parts of it, as she repeated them to herself, moved her to tears. A new sullenness was added to the previous listlessness of her demeanour. She parted from Mr. Loftus with studied indifference.

Mr. Loftus missed her, not altogether unpleasantly, when she left him. It was the first time that she had been a day away from him since their marriage. Life was certainly very tranquil without her. He wrote her a charming little letter every day of the three days she was away.

Doll was with him on business. Now that Sibyl was absent, something of the old affection and confidence returned between them, which shrank away in her presence; but not quite all. At times, as they were talking, the younger man longed to break down the slight, almost imperceptible barrier that his stupid untimely silence had raised. But he could not do it. He could not take the plunge. Mr. Loftus, however, who would not have done such a thing for worlds, unwittingly gave him a push.

'The spring coppice wants thinning,' he said to Doll the third morning. 'We will go up and mark the trees this afternoon.'

'I am going away to-day,' said Doll sullenly.

'Stay another day,' said Mr. Loftus. 'Mrs. Gresley tells me that the sight of her happy home, and Mr. Gresley, and the church-tower as viewed from the spare bedroom of the Vicarage, have proved a turning-point in the lives of many wild young men. Stay another day, Doll, and I will emulate Mrs. Gresley. It will do you good.'

'Uncle George,' stammered the young man with sudden anger, 'will you never, never understand? Have you forgotten that it is not a year ago since I told you—in this very room—and you said you would help me. I can't meet Sibyl; and—and she is coming back to-day. I tried in the winter, and—it was a failure.'

Mr. Loftus had momentarily forgotten Sibyl, as he had done once before when she was ill.

' I beg your pardon, Doll,' he said, his pale face reddening. 'I ought to have remembered.'

There was a constrained silence.

' It need not come between us,' said Mr. Loftus at last. ' You must not let it do that.'

' I can't help it,' said Doll. ' It does. It must.'

' Sibyl's happiness,' said Mr. Loftus sadly, 'seems to be a costly article. A great deal has been spent upon it, apparently without making it secure. If we have any real regard for her, we must manage to save that between us, Doll, whatever else goes by the board.'

' What do you take me for?' said Doll fiercely.

' A good man,' said Mr. Loftus, ' and the person I care for most in the world.'

Sibyl's letter to Mr. Loftus was never written. At least it was written, as, indeed, were several, and read over and retouched at night in her own room ; but even the best of the assortment remained unposted. Sibyl brought back her wan face and limp figure to Wilderleigh a few hours after Doll had left it, and heard with bitterness that he had been staying there. She had pictured to herself Mr. Loftus alone, missing her at every moment of the day, realizing the withdrawal of the sunshine of her presence. This was a 'high jump,' on the bar of which, it must be owned, even her practised imagination caught its toe. And now she found that Doll had been with him all the time— Doll, whom he cared for more than for his wife. He had not missed her, after all. Probably he and Doll had been discussing her. She had been jealous of Doll ever since she had seen Mr. Loftus take his arm during her first visit to Wilderleigh before she was married.

Her jealousy revived now. For the remainder of the day Sibyl met Mr. Loftus with averted eyes and monosyllabic answers, rehearsing in her mind parting scenes with him which were to prove more poignantly distressing to him than the best of the letters, and in which he was to appeal in vain (imagination caught its toe once more) against her irrevocable determination to leave for ever one who had married her for other motives than love.

She could see herself in evening dress, pale as the jasmine flower in her breast, mournful but unflinching, withdrawing her hand, and saying, in reply to the moving

representation which he would of course
make of his loneliness :

'You have Doll !'

She decided that she would not say
more than that.   No reproach should pass
her lips.

"You have Doll !'

What words for a young wife to be
forced to use to her husband !   Her hands
clenched in an agony of self-pity.   What a
cruel situation was hers !

So Sibyl walked in her waking dream,
and her husband watched her.

'Is it the body that is ill, or is it the
mind ?' he asked himself.

Later in the day the doctor's letter to
himself—Mr. Loftus had written to him
asking for a frank statement of Sibyl's
condition—confirmed his worst fears for
her.

' Mrs. Loftus's health is endangered, not by her recent illness, of which no trace appears, but by some anxiety. She does not deny that she is suffering from great depression. Unless that anxiety, whatever it may be, can be removed, her morbid condition, if prolonged, will give rise to grave apprehension as to her future.'

Mr. Loftus had heard something very like this before—about nine months ago. He had removed a mountain in order to remove with it the first cause of her unhappiness, and now unhappiness had reappeared. No one had guessed—no one had been allowed to guess—what an effort his marriage had been to him. And it had availed nothing. He dropped the letter into the fire, and, as he did so, exhaustion and an intense weariness of life laid hold upon him. He knew well the touch of those stern hands, but this evening, as he sat alone in the library, it seemed to him as if he had never endured their full pressure until now.

CHAPTER XIII.

'O World, O Life, O Time.
O these last steps on which I climb.'

SHELLEY.

FOR those who do not sleep, life has two
sides—the side of night as well as day—
and the heaviest hour of the day or night
is the hour before the dawn, when the
night-lamp totters and dies, and the ashen
light of another day falls like despair on
the familiar articles of furniture, the chairs,
the table, the wardrobe, which have been
up all night like ourselves, taking the im-
print of our exhaustion through the inter-
minable hours, and which look older and

more haggard than ever in the changed light which brings nor change nor rest.

Those who sleep at night, for whom each day is not divided by a gulf of pain, who look upon the darkness as a time of rest, and the morning as a time of waking, know one side of life, perhaps, as the passers-by in the street know one side of the hospital as they skirt it—the outside wall.

Mr. Loftus slept ill, and the night after Sibyl's return he woke early. The gray light was just showing above the white blinds as he had seen it so many, many times. Would the morning ever come, he wondered, when he should no longer open his eyes upon the dawn, when 'these last steps' should be climbed, and effort would cease, and weariness might lie down and cease also ?

The premonitory tremor, the shudder of coming illness, laid its hand upon him, and with it came that physical recoil of the flesh from solitude before which the strongest will goes down.

Involuntarily he got up and went to Sibyl's room. He opened the door noiselessly and looked in.

The room felt deserted. He went up to the bed ; it was empty. A great fear fell upon him. Had she left him ? Poor, poor child ! had she left him, as that other wife had left him in the half-forgotten past, buried beneath so many years ? Can any man whose wife has forsaken him ever quite forget that he has once been deserted, that the road which leads away from him has known a woman's footsteps, and another may walk in it ? He stood still and listened. The spirit had over-mastered the flesh. All suffering had vanished.

From the next room, Sibyl's sitting-room, which opened out of her bedroom, a faint sound came. He noiselessly crossed, and looked through the half-open door, and thanked God.

Sibyl was lying on her face on the polished floor in her night-gown, moaning and sobbing, a white blot upon the dark boards.

He had seen her lie like that once before, among the bracken in the park, in the entire abandonment of young despair. The vague suspicion of many weeks dropped its disguise, and stood revealed, an awful figure between them, between the old man in his gray hair and the young, young wife.

He withdrew stealthily, regained his

own room, and sat down in the armchair.

That passion of tears could flow from
one source only. He knew Sibyl well
enough to know that she had no tears,
no strong emotion, for anything except
that which affected her own personal
happiness. Her slight nature could not
reach to impersonal love, any more than
it could reach to righteous anger. All
this apparent failure of health and listlessness had a mental cause, as he had
always feared, as he now knew for certain.
She was unhappy.

'She has ceased to love me,' said
Mr. Loftus to himself, 'and she is in
despair. Doll loves her, and she has
found it out. Those tears are for Doll.'

There was a long pause of thought.

He started at the remembrance that

she was probably still lying on the floor in her thin night-gown.

He got up, and tapped distinctly at the door of her bedroom. At first there was no reply, but after the second time there was a slight hurried movement and a faint 'Come in.' He went in. She had crept back into bed, as he had hoped she would at the sound of his tap.

'May I have your salts?' he said, taking them from the dressing-table. 'I have waked with a headache.'

'Can I do anything for it?' she asked, but without moving, her miserable eyes following his thin, gaunt figure in its gray dressing-gown.

'Nothing, my dear, except forgive me for disturbing you.'

'I was not asleep,' said Sibyl, yielding to the impulse, irresistible to some women, to approach the subject which they are trying to conceal.

He took the salts, and went back to his own room, closing the door carefully. But he did not use them. He sighed heavily as he sat down again in the old armchair in which he had so often watched the light grow behind the Welsh hills.

There was another pause of thought, and he remembered again Doll's confession of the day before.

'Poor children!' he said—'poor children!'

And he remembered his own youth and its devastating passions, and the woman whom he had loved in middle life, and how nearly once—how nearly—— And he and she had been stronger than Doll and Sibyl.

'God forgive me!' he said; 'I meant well.'

There was another pause.

'I knew her love could not last,' his mind went on. 'It was too extravagant, and it had no foundation. But I thought it would last my time, and it has not. I have outlived it; I am in the way.'

Mr. Loftus had never willingly been in the way of anyone before. His tact had so far saved him. But a kind intention had betrayed him at last.

'I am in the way,' he repeated, 'and I am fond of them both, and I think they are both fond of me. But they will come to hate me.'

The light was strong and white now, and a butterfly on the window-sill, that had mistaken spring for summer, waked, and began to beat its wings against the pane.

He rose wearily, and opened the old-

fashioned window wide upon its hinges.
The butterfly flew away into the spring
morning.

'My other butterfly,' he said—'my
pretty butterfly, who mistook the spring
for summer, breaking your heart against
the prison windows of my worn-out life—
I will release you, too !'

He took up the little silver flask that
always stood on his dressing-table at night
and lived in his pocket by day, and which
contained the only remedy which a great
doctor could find for his attacks of the
heart, by means of which he had been till
now kept in life.

'I have a right to do it,' he said. 'I
can only help them by going away. And
if I am in the wrong, upon my head
be it.'

He checked himself in the act of empty-

ing the contents of the flask into the dead
fire.

'A right?' he said. 'What right have
I to shirk the consequences of my own
actions? what right to be a coward?
No; I will not go away until I receive
permission to do so. I will stay while it is
required of me.'

He sighed heavily, and replaced the
flask upon the dressing-table.

'Patience,' he said. 'I thought I had
seen the last of you. I am tired of you.
But, nevertheless, I must put up with you
a little longer.'

CHAPTER XIV.

'As the water is dried upon sands, so a life flieth
back to the dust.'—SIR ALFRED LYALL.

How Sibyl spent the morning that followed
she never knew. She dared not go out of
doors. The world of spring, with the new
breath of life in it, mocked her. The
song of the birds hurt her. She felt as if
she should scream outright if she saw the
may-blossom against the sky. She wandered aimlessly about the house, and at
last crept back to her own room and lay
down on her bed, and turned her face to
the wall.

13—2

The day went on.   Her maid brought
her soup, and drew down the blinds, and
was pettishly dismissed.

The afternoon came.   They were mowing the grass on the terrace on the south
front.   The faint scent of newly-cut grass
came in through the open window, and
seemed, through the senses, to reach some
acute nerve of the brain.   She moaned,
and buried her face in the pillows.   Presently the mowing ceased, and everything
became very silent.   A bluebottle fly,
pressed for time, rushed in, made the
circuit of the room, and rushed out again.

Far away in the other wing, on the
ground-floor, she heard the library door
open.   She knew Mr. Loftus's slow, even
step.   It crossed the hall; it entered the
orangery;   it   came   out   through   the
orangery door, down the stone steps to

the terrace below her window. She could hear his step on the gravel outside in the crisp air. Crack gave a short bark in recognition of the spring, and satisfaction that the long morning of arranging papers and the afternoon of letter-writing were at last over.

The steps dwindled and died away into the sunny silence. It seemed to Sibyl's overwrought mind that he was walking slowly out of her life, and that unless she made haste to follow him she would lose him altogether. With a sudden revulsion of feeling, she sprang to her feet, and put on her hat and shoes. Then she braved the spring, and went swiftly out.

* * * * *

A great tranquillity had fallen upon Mr. Loftus. He had made up his mind. After a turn along the terrace, he and

Crack went into the little wood near the gardens, and sat down under the pink horse - chestnut - tree, just blushing into flower. It would have been difficult to put the arrangement into words, but there was a tacit understanding between the husband and wife that when Mr. Loftus sat under that particular tree he did not mind being interrupted. Sibyl generally fluttered out to him after he had been there a few minutes, though the wood was out of sight of the windows. And he waited for her to come to him now.

Spring had returned at last. But you might have walked through the wood and not known she was there : have seen only the naked trees, and the gray twigs of the alder, bleached white where the rabbits had bitten them in the frost. But if you had stopped to listen and look as Mr.

Loftus did, you would have seen and
heard her; seen her in the blue haze, and
the mystery of change that lurked among
the gray twigs, and in the rare primroses
among the brown leaves; heard her in the
persistent double-tongue of the chiff-chaff,
and, not near at hand, but two trees away,
in the ripple of the goldfinch, with a little
question at the end of it. Is it a hint of
immortality, that haunting desire and ex-
pectation of happiness which comes with
the primroses, that longing for some future
year when the spring shall bring with it
no heartache, the autumn no contrition; of
another year, somewhere in the future,
when the ills of life will be done away?
Mr. Loftus looked straight in front of him,
and his face took an expression as of one
whose eyes are on a goal where even
patience itself, so visible in every line of

his quiet face, will at last with other burdens be laid aside.

She saw him before he saw her, as she came towards him. Her heart went out to him wistfully and passionately by turns. She longed to turn to him as a young wife turns to a young husband, and cry her heart out on his breast, and be petted, and caressed, and comforted. But she dared not. Whatever besides she was ignorant of, she had learnt certain things about her husband, and one of them was that she must never show her devotion unasked. And she was seldom asked. Her life was a constant repression of its greatest, its only real affection.

As she came towards him he roused himself and smiled at her. She sat down by him in silence. He had a single primrose in the buttonhole of his coat, and he took it out and drew it very gently through the Russian embroidery on her bodice.

'When I was young, Sibyl,' he said, 'I was convinced, and the conviction has never wholly left me, that flowers are God's thoughts which He sows broadcast in the hearts of all alike. But we will have none of them, and they drop unheeded to the ground. But the faithful earth receives them—thoughts despised and rejected of us—and nurses them in her bosom, and they come forth transfigured. And that is why, when we see them again, we love them so much, and feel akin to them.'

Her locked hands trembled on her knee.

'It must have been a beautiful thought that could turn into a lily,' he went on, noting, but ignoring, her emotion. 'I wonder, if it had fallen into a poet's heart, what it would have grown into. Nothing more beautiful, I think. And I know the primroses are first love. I have felt sure of that always. I wonder, my Sibyl, when there is so much in your heart for me, that there are any left to come out in the woods ; but there are a few, you see, among the brown leaves.'

'They will soon be over,' said Sibyl, turning her head away.

'Yes,' said Mr. Loftus, with a gentleness which was new to Sibyl, and he was always gentle. 'They will die presently, as first love dies. But nevertheless it is a beautiful gift while it lasts, and we must not grieve because, like the primroses, it cannot last in flower *for ever.* I have lived through so many feelings, Sibyl, I have seen so many die which seemed immortal, that I have long since ceased to count on the permanence of any.'

He leant towards her, and for the first time he took her slender hands and kissed them. It was as if he were readjusting his position towards her, reassuring her of his trust and confidence and sympathy, supporting her in some great trouble. She leaned her forehead against his shoulder, and a sense of comfort came across her desolation, as if she were leaning her faint soul against his soul. He put his arm round her, and drew her closer to him.

' My darling!' he said, and there was an emotion in his voice which she had never heard in it before. Her hat had slipped off, and he passed his hand very tenderly over her hair.

Sibyl's over-strained nerves relaxed. Some of the craving of her heart and its long yearning was stilled by the touch of his hand. Ah! he loved her, after all—certainly he loved her. Doll was right, after all. How foolish she had been to cry all night! Certainly he loved her.

She could not speak. She could not weep. She could only lean against him. She had never known him like this before. It was this that she had always wanted, all her life, long before she had ever met him.

'You have been so good to me,' he went on, 'from the first day of our married life when I was ill. Do you remember? And I know that your dear love and kindness will not fail me while I live. I thank and bless you for all you have given me, your whole spring of primroses; and now that spring is passing, as it must, Sibyl, as it must, not by your fault, take comfort,

and when other feelings come into your
heart, as they have come in, do not
reproach yourself, do not cut me to the
heart by grieving, but remember that I
understand, and that my love and honour
and gratitude can never change towards
you, and that I too was young once : as
young as—Doll, and there is no need
for you and him to be so miserable.
It will only be — like a—long engagement.'

As the drift of his words gradually
became clear to her, Sibyl insensibly
shrank back as from an abyss before her
feet. But in another moment she took in
their whole meaning. She pushed him
from her with sudden violence, and stood
before him, her hands clenched, her eyes
blazing, her slender figure shaking with
passion.

'How dare you!' she stammered. 'How dare you insult me?'

He put out his hand feebly, and she struck it down.

'What is Doll to me?' she went on, 'to me, *your wife!* Oh, will you never, never understand that I love you, that I worship you, that I care for nothing in the whole world but you, and that I cried all night because you married me out of pity?' Sibyl wrung her hands. 'Oh! how dared you do it, how dared you swear to love me before God, if you did not, if you could not? I am too miserable. I cannot bear it—I cannot bear it!'

He sat like one stunned. His hand went to his heart.

In a moment her arms were round him, and his head was on her shoulder.

'Forgive,' he repeated over and over

again, between the long - drawn gasps
which shook him from head to foot.

And then the battle for life began.

She found his little flask in his pocket,
and managed to make him swallow the
contents.

He struggled, but she upheld him. Her
strength was as the strength of ten.

At last, all in a moment, the struggle
ceased, and a light came into his fixed eyes
of awe and thankfulness, and—was it joy?

He did not move. He did not speak.
His whole being seemed absorbed in that
of some vast enfolding presence.

She called him wildly by name.

He trembled, and his troubled eyes,
with all the light blown out of them,
wandered back to seek hers. Death
looked at her through them. He saw
her as across a gulf. He recognised her.

He remembered.   He had hoped that when he came to die it might be quietly, without a scene, but it was not to be.   He made a last effort.

'Not for pity—for——' he gasped, his ebbing breath winnowing the air.   But Death cut short the lie faltering on his lips, and his head fell suddenly forward on her breast.   She held him closely to her, murmuring incoherent words of love and tenderness, such as she had never dared to speak while he had ears to hear.

*   *   *   *   *

How long she had knelt beside him, holding him in her arms, the frightened servants, who at last found them after sunset, never knew.   And when they came to lay him in his coffin, they saw on one of the thin folded hands a faint blue mark, as from a blow.

POSTSCRIPT.

SIBYL was an inconsolable widow. Her grief reached a depth which placed her beyond the succour of human sympathy, and Lady Pierpoint, who had lost her young husband in her youth, was felt to take a superficial view of Sibyl's bereavement.

She shut herself up at Wilderleigh for a year and refused comfort, and then suddenly married Doll, the only man except Mr. Gresley whom she had allowed to see her during her widowhood.

In rather less than a month after her

14

marriage with him she made the interesting discovery that he was the only man in the world who really understood her. His gift of platitude, harmonizing as it did with hers, was an inexhaustible source of admiration to her. She was wont to say in confidence to her woman friends, that, devotedly as she had loved her first husband, she had found her ideal in her second one; and that it was to Doll she owed the real development of her character, a subject in which she took great interest.

For some years, while her daughter remained an only child, she was passionately devoted to her. But when her son was born she ceased to take much interest in the little girl, who was by this time rather spoilt, and consequently tiresome. Doll, who proved exemplary in domestic life, took to her when Sibyl forgot her, and became deeply attached to her. Later in life Sibyl became inconsolably jealous of her daughter.

THE END.

BILLING AND SONS, PRINTERS, GUILDFORD.

NOVELS FROM
MR. EDWARD ARNOLD'S LIST.

By the Author of ' The Red Badge of Courage.'

GEORGE'S MOTHER.

By STEPHEN CRANE.

Cloth, 2s.

Saturday Review.

' From first to last it goes with immense vigour and sympathy. But the story must be read for its power to be understood ; quota-tion fails, for the simple reason that it is a bare story and nothing beyond. Apart from its distinctive qualities, English readers will welcome this book as an indication of the growth of a real and inde-pendent critical method across the Atlantic, side by side and directing really original work.'

Athenæum.

' A striking scene of the relations, in a rough world, between a boy and his mother.'

Speaker.

' Stephen Crane proved conclusively in " The Red Badge of Courage " his possession of an extraordinary power of vivid and accurate vision expressed with startling poignancy of phrase ; and in his later production, " George's Mother," we find the same rugged directness and almost savage intensity, the same contempt for con. ventional graces of style, and the love for violent colouring, which marked his previous work.'

Daily Chronicle.

' The gradual progress of deterioration in George Kelcey is very briefly but very cleverly and convincingly set out.'

St. James's Gazette.

' It is a *tour de force* of description and analysis, this terrible scene of George's debauch—not in the least laboured, or Zolaistic, or photographic, but amazingly actual, and lightened with a grim sense of humour.'

By the Author of 'Into the Highways and Hedges.'

WORTH WHILE.

By F. F. MONTRÉSOR,

Author of 'Into the Highways and Hedges,' 'The One Who
Looked on.'

Crown 8vo., cloth, 2s. 6d.

Academy.

'The quiet excellence of Miss Montrésor's little book may likely
enough cause it to lie unnoticed among its thrilling companions.
There is, none the less, more of art and literature in two short
sketches than one is likely to meet with again in a hurry. If inferior
work, gaudily bedraped, gets all the encores, in the shape of many
editions, I cannot think she will greatly care. Such work as hers
only comes, as the proverb has it, by prayer and fasting. And she
will receive ungrudging praise from those who revere sterling merit,
and respect labour at once unobtrusive, competent, sincere.'

Guardian.

' " Worth While " is a real idyll of a life's sacrifice, most sweetly
and touchingly told.'

Glasgow Herald.

'Both the stories in this volume are of very superior quality.
The characters are distinctly original, and the workmanship is
admirable.'

Manchester Mercury.

'Although the two stories contained in the present volume are
comparatively short, they serve to display the author's peculiar gifts
n a striking manner.'

Liverpool Courier.

'Two most pathetic and beautiful stories make up this little
volume. The writer is to be congratulated on the delicate beauty
of her stories.'

By the Author of 'The Apotheosis of Mr. Tyrawley.'

A MASK AND A MARTYR.

By E. LIVINGSTON PRESCOTT.

One vol., crown 8vo., cloth, 6s.

Westminster Gazette.

' This s an undeniably clever book. A picture of self-sacrifice so complete and so enduring is a rare picture in fiction, and has rarely been more ably or more finely drawn. This singular and pathetic story is told all through with remarkable restraint, and shows a strength and skill of execution which place its author high among the novel-writers of the day.'

Daily Telegraph.

' There is no doubt that this is a striking book. The story it has to tell is thoroughly original and unconventional, while the manner of telling shows much restrained power.'

Spectator.

' Mr. Prescott has evidently a future before him.'

Pall Mall Gazette.

Mr. Prescott has given us a clever and an interesting book. We have seldom read of such superhuman courage, such transcendent love, as Mr. Prescott has shown us in his masterly picture of Captain Cosmo Harradyne, of the Fighting Hussars. A story which we confidently, nay, earnestly, recommend to our readers ; they will thank us for doing so.'

National Observer.

' A book which has much cleverness of treatment, an excellent style, a great deal of interest, a high ideal, and a real pathos. Perhaps it is not necessary to add that a novel of which so much can be said is one greatly above the common run of fiction. The book should be, and we have no doubt will be, read with real interest by many people.'

'One of the best stories of the season.'—*Daily Chronicle.*

HADJIRA,

A TURKISH LOVE STORY.

By ADALET.

One volume, crown 8vo., cloth, 6s.

Speaker.

'Certainly one of the most interesting and valuable works of fiction issued from the press for a long time past. Even if we were to regard the book as an ordinary novel, we could commend it heartily ; but its great value lies in the fact that it reveals to us a hidden world, and does so with manifest fidelity. But the reader must learn for himself the lesson which this remarkable and fascinating book teaches.'

Daily Chronicle.

'A Turkish love story written in excellent English by a young Ottoman lady, would be a book worth reading, if only as a curiosity ; but when, as in this instance, it is of uncommon merit and originality, it is particularly welcome. It is deeply interesting, fascinatingly so. It is as a picture of family life in Turkey that this book is so interesting, possibly because the picture it provides is unexpectedly agreeable. As a study of Turkish life in our times, when Western civilization is beginning to penetrate into the seclusion of the harem, this book is a valuable contribution to contemporary literature. It is a well-merited compliment to its author to say of " Hadjira " that it is one of the best stories of the season.'

Pall Mall Gazette.

'An interesting and readable book.'

St. James's Gazette.

'The book is excellently written. As a clearly truthful account of modern Turkish life, from the woman's point of view, it is as valuable as it is interesting. We shall hope to have more from the same pen.'

Guardian.

'A curiously interesting bit of work.'

A RELUCTANT EVANGELIST.

By ALICE SPINNER.

Author of ' Lucilla,' ' A Study in Colour,' etc.

Crown 8vo., 1 vol., 6s.

Saturday Review.

' " A Reluctant Evangelist" is as good as its predecessor " Lucilla," which we were glad to be able to praise last year. The West Indies, with their "colour problem," their weird romance and undercurrent of horror, will last a long time as background for new stories.'

Glasgow Herald.

' It is into the wonderland of the West Indies that Miss Spinner takes us : into a region of hot sunshine, of blue sky, of sparkling sea. All the stories are excellent, and will repay perusal.'

Pall Mall Gazette.

' Good, too, is Miss Spinner's budget of short stories. " Buckra Tommie " is an exquisitely pathetic story. The writer is evidently at home in the South Seas, and with the out-of-the-way humanity she meets there.'

Irish Times.

' A charming little series of stories. They are very daintily written, and although the incidents upon which they turn are not always very striking, they are at all events novel, and they have been conceived with much dramatic power.'

Cape Times.

' These short stories are all distinctly good.'

Englishman.

' We can strongly recommend these stories. They are varied and interesting, and have a distinct literary merit.'

INTERLUDES.

By MAUD OXENDEN.

One volume, crown 8vo., 6s.

Scotsman.

'The writer is to be congratulated on the strength with which she portrays men and women, and describes the passions of love or of grief that sometimes fill the mind. There are other personages in these pages, whose experiences of love and joy and grief are under other circumstances than those indicated ; but if the writer had depicted none other than the three personages that appear in the tragic scene in London she would have scored a distinct success. An admirably-written book.'

Sheffield Telegraph.

'We have not read anything so tenderly touched with pathos, and at the same time so delicately told, for a very long time. Indeed, " Interludes " is about as good a piece of literary work of its class as we could wish to read, and is worth a high place in the works which appeal to the emotional in our nature.'

Bradford Observer.

'The stories evince a considerable and disciplined faculty of invention which, though it produces situations of intense interest, never becomes riotous or extravagant. We will close our too brief note with an expression of the pleasure we have felt in reading these chaste and beautiful fancies.'

Guardian.

'There is much that is both clever and original in Miss Oxenden's " Interludes." There is often very genuine pathos, and nearly all the volume is interesting.'.

TWENTY-SECOND THOUSAND.

STEPHEN REMARX.

THE STORY OF A VENTURE IN ETHICS.

BY THE HON. AND REV. JAMES ADDERLEY.

Small 8vo., elegantly bound, 3s. 6d. ; paper, 1s.

Daily Telegraph.

' Written with a vigour, warmth, and sincerity which cannot fail to captivate the reader's attention and command his respect.'

Saturday Review.

' Let us express our thankfulness at encountering, for once in a way, an author who can amuse us.'

Star.

' The book is charmingly written.'

Guardian.

' Not only do we agree with Mr. Adderley in his general objects, and in many of his fundamental principles, but we believe that the path of reform lies very much in the direction to which he has pointed.'

Daily Chronicle.

' The story is one of a novel kind, and many people will find it interesting and very suggestive.'

Rock.

' A little but very notable volume.'

Record.

' A little book, but one of which much will be heard.'

DAVE'S SWEETHEART.

By MARY GAUNT.

One vol., 8vo., cloth, 3s. 6d.

Spectator.

' It is interesting to watch the literature which is coming over to
us from Australia, a portion of which is full of promise, but we may
safely say that of all the novels that have been laid before readers in
this country, " Dave's Sweetheart," in a literary point of view and
as a finished production, takes a higher place than any that has yet
appeared. From the opening scene to the closing page we have no
hesitation in predicting that not a word will be skipped even by the
most *blasé* of novel readers.'

Daily Telegraph.

' In every respect one of the most powerful and impressive novels
of the year.'

Tablet.

' Essentially a strong book. The writer has a wonderfully clean
way of describing the elemental facts of life, and lets her plummet-
line go down deep into the depths of human tears. The book is of
interest down to the last line.'

Weekly Sun.

' The narrative is throughout animated, and rises occasionally to
heights of great dramatic power, whilst the picture of life in the
diggings is delineated in a way that compels admiration.'

Morning Post.

' The action is rapid and well-developed, the incidents exciting,
as becomes the nature of the subject, and the human interest un-
usually deep.'

Times.

' A vigorous and dramatic story of the early gold-digging days in
Victoria. " Dave's Sweetheart " is a good story.'

Guardian.

' Many books of Australian life have come before us lately, and
to none of them are we inclined to give more honest praise than to
" Dave's Sweetheart." '

Speaker.

' Alike from a dramatic and a literary point of view, " Dave's
Sweetheart " is admirably told, with restraint and with distinction.'

TOMMY ATKINS.

A Tale of the Ranks.

By ROBERT BLATCHFORD,

Author of ' A Son of the Forge,' ' Merrie England,' etc.

Second Edition.   Crown 8vo., cloth, 6s.

Bradford Observer.
' A splendid narrative of the barrack life of the rank and file.'

Eastern Morning News.
' There is not a dull page in the book.'

Glasgow Herald.
' Most vigorous and picturesque sketches of barrack life.'

Scotsman.
' Entertaining throughout, and reveals high literary ability.'

Dundee Advertiser.
' A really vivacious book ; the incidents are so well selected that the reader never wearies from start to finish.'

Liverpool Post.
' The book is both clever and amusing.'

Broad Arrow.
' For this well-conceived, well-written, and well-informed little story we have little but commendation to offer.'

THE BAYONET THAT CAME HOME.

By N. WYNN WILLIAMS,

Author of ' Tales of Modern Greece.'

Crown 8vo., 3s. 6d.

Dundee Advertiser.
' Well worth perusing.'

National Observer.
' Mr. Williams's story of modern Greece throws a curious light on her corrupt politics, on petty oppression, and on the conscription, with its attendant hardships to the peasant population.'

Glasgow Herald.
' A powerfully-written and vivid little story.'

LOVE-LETTERS OF A WORLDLY WOMAN.

By MRS. W. K. CLIFFORD,

Author of ' Aunt Anne,' ' Mrs. Keith's Crime,' etc.

Cloth, 2s. 6d.

Queen.

' One of the cleverest books that ever a woman wrote.'

Morning Post.

' It is that *rara avis*—a volume characterized by knowledge of human nature and brightened by refined wit.'

World.

' A book that will gladden the hearts of those who love literature for its own sake.'

Review of Reviews.

' Many writers have pictured to us a woman, but none more successfully than Mrs. Clifford, whose Madge Brooke stands forth distinct and almost flesh and blood—a human document.'

ON THE THRESHOLD.

By ISABELLA O. FORD,

Author of ' Miss Blake, of Monksbalton.'

Cloth, 3s. 6d.

Guardian.

' It is a relief to turn from many of the novels that come before us to Miss Ford's true, penetrating, and sympathetic description of the lives of some of the women of our day.'

Bradford Observer.

' Those who have followed and admired Miss Ford's active social and political work will be interested in this latest work of hers, and will understand its special characteristics. It only remains to be added that the literary workmanship of the book is excellent.'

Hearth and Home.

' A decidedly clever book.'

MISTHER O'RYAN.

An Incident in the History of a Nation.

By EDWARD McNULTY.

Small 8vo., elegantly bound, 3s. 6d.

National Observer.

' "Ould Paddy" and the "poor dark cratur" are as pathetic figures as any we have met with in recent romance, and would alone stamp their creator as a writer of real force and originality.'

Pall Mall Gazette.

'An extremely well-written satire of the possibilities of blarney and brag.'

Bookman.

'An Irish story of far more than ordinary ability.'

Church Times.

'A sad story, but full of racy Irish wit.'

Yorkshire Post.

' It is a book to circulate everywhere, a book which, by its pathos and its power, its simplicity and its vivid truth, will impress the mind as the logic and the reasoning of the statesman too rarely do.'

ORMISDAL.

By the EARL OF DUNMORE, F.R.G.S.,

Author of 'The Pamirs.'

One vol., cloth, 6s.

Glasgow Herald.

' In this breezy and entertaining novel Lord Dunmore has given us a very readable and racy story of the life that centres in a Highland shooting, about the end of August.'

St. James's Gazette.

' The impression left on the mind after laying down "Ormisdal" is that Lord Dunmore is a remarkably lucky man to lead such a pleasant life among such charming people and in such charming places, and that everybody will be delighted to hear from him again, when he has more of the same sort to tell us, whether he wraps it up in a book of personal anecdote or a novel.'

TWO FAMOUS FRENCH NOVELS.

THE TUTOR'S SECRET.

(*LE SECRET DU PRÉCEPTEUR.*)

Translated from the French of VICTOR CHERBULIEZ.

One volume, crown 8vo., cloth, 6s.

Daily Chronicle.

'M. Cherbuliez is to be congratulated on having found a trans-
lator who has done justice to him, and to do justice to M. Cherbuliez
is no mean achievement, for he is one of the most artistic and
delightful of modern French novelists. He is also one of the few
whose works may be safely left lying about where the young person
is prone to penetrate. In "The Tutor's Secret" all his finest
qualities are to be found.'

Manchester Guardian.

'An admirable translation of a delightful novel. Those who
have not read it in French must hasten to read it in English.'

Westminster Gazette.

'If Victor Cherbuliez did not already possess a great reputation
his latest production would have been quite sufficient to secure him
renown as a novelist. From the first line to the last we recognise a
master hand at work, and there is not a page that even the veriest
skimmer will care to pass over.'

THE MYSTERY OF THE RUE SOLY.

From the French of II. DE BALZAC, by LADY KNUTSFORD.

One volume, 8vo., cloth, 3s. 6d.

Spectator.

'To place a first-rate foreign novel in reach of those whose
education does not enable them to enjoy it in the original is to con-
fer a real boon upon them ; and everyone who is not a French
scholar has much cause to be grateful to Lady Knutsford for the
capital translation of Balzac's renowned Ferragus.'

Scotsman.

'Lady Knutsford's translation is excellent.'

Speaker.

'Admirably translated.'